A TOMB FOR BORIS DAVIDOVICH

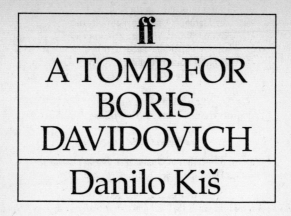

A TOMB FOR BORIS DAVIDOVICH

Danilo Kiš

faber and faber

LONDON · BOSTON

First published in the USA in 1978
by Harcourt Brace Jovanovich, Inc.
First published in Great Britain in 1985
by Faber and Faber Limited
3 Queen Square London WC1N 3AU

Printed in Great Britain by
Redwood Burn Limited Trowbridge Wiltshire

English translation of *Grobnica za Borisa Davidoviča*
© Harcourt Brace Jovanovich, Inc. 1978

British Library Cataloguing in Publication Data

Kiš, Danilo
A tomb for Boris Davidovich.
I. Title
891.8′235   PG1419.21.I8
ISBN 0–571–13736–9

CONTENTS

THE KNIFE WITH THE ROSEWOOD HANDLE

FOR MIRKO KOVAČ

The story that I am about to tell, a story born in doubt and perplexity, has only the misfortune (some call it the fortune) of being true: it was recorded by the hands of honorable people and reliable witnesses. But to be true in the way its author dreams about, it would have to be told in Romanian, Hungarian, Ukrainian, or Yiddish; or, rather, in a mixture of all these languages. Then, by the logic of chance and of murky, deep, unconscious happenings, through the consciousness of the narrator, there would flash also a Russian word or two, now a tender one like *telyatina*, now a hard one like *kinjal*. If the narrator, therefore, could reach the unattainable, terrifying moment of Babel, the humble pleadings and awful beseechings of Hanna Krzyzewska would resound in Romanian, in Polish, in Ukrainian (as if her death were only the consequence of some great and fatal misunderstanding), and then just before the death rattle and final calm her incoherence would turn into the prayer for the dead, spoken in Hebrew, the language of being and dying.

A POSITIVE HERO

Miksha (let's call him that for now) could sew on a button in ten seconds. Light a match and hold it between your fingers; between the time you light it and the time it burns your fingers, Miksha would have sewn a button on an officer's uniform. Reb Mendel, for whom Miksha worked as an apprentice, couldn't believe his eyes. He adjusted his glasses, took out a match, and said in Yiddish, "Come on, do it again, Herr Micksat." Reb Mendel smiled as he watched Miksha thread the needle again. Then suddenly he threw the match out the window and spat on his fingers. Miksha, who had already sewn the button on Herr Antonescu's uniform, said triumphantly, "Reb Mendel, one single match could blow up all the oil fields of Ploesti." While he imagined the distant future illuminated by a huge blaze, Reb Mendel, with two fingers still damp, quickly pulled at the button on the uniform and twisted it as if it were the neck of a chicken. "Herr Micksat," he said, "if you didn't have such foolish thoughts, you could become an excellent craftsman. Do you know that the oil fields of Ploesti are estimated to have several million gallons of crude oil?" "It'll be a wonderful flame, Reb Mendel," said Miksha enigmatically.

THE OUTWITTING OF REB MENDEL

Miksha didn't become a master craftsman. For two more years he sewed on buttons at Reb Mendel's, listening to his Talmudic reasonings, and then was forced to leave, sent off with a curse. One day in the spring of the notable year 1925, Reb Mendel complained that one of his Cochin hens had disappeared. "Reb Mendel," said Miksha, "look for the thief among the Jews." Reb Mendel understood the force of the insult and for some time didn't mention his Cochin hen. Miksha was also silent; he was waiting for Reb Mendel to conquer his pride. The old man struggled within himself, each day sacrificing a hen on the altar of his Talmudic haughtiness. With a stick in his hand, he kept vigil in the chicken coop until dawn, frightening away a skunk by barking like a dog. At dawn he fell asleep, and another hen disappeared from the chicken coop. "Let the great Righteous One smite me, He who said that all living creatures are equally worthy of His care and mercy," said Reb Mendel on the ninth day. "Is it possible that one Cochin hen worth at least five chevronets is equal to a skunk who robs the poor and stinks far and wide?" "It isn't, Reb Mendel," said Miksha. "A Cochin hen worth at least five chevronets can't be compared with a stinking skunk." He said no more. He waited for the skunk to destroy what it could destroy, and to prove to Reb Mendel that his Talmudic prattle about the equality of all God's creatures was worthless until justice was achieved on earth by earthly means. On the eleventh day Reb Mendel, exhausted by futile vigils, swollen and red-eyed, his hair full of feathers, stood in front of Miksha and began to beat his breast. "Herr Micksat, help me!" "All right, Reb Mendel," said Miksha. "Brush off your caftan and take the feathers out of your hair. Leave this matter to me."

THE TRAP

The trap that Miksha slapped together was a distant replica of those his grandfather used to make long ago in Bukovina: a murky and nostalgic memory. Apart from this, it was a simple box made of hard beech planks, with a lid that opened from the outside but not from the inside. As bait he placed an egg that (as he had made absolutely certain) already held a Cochin chicken, rotting as if in a coffin. In the morning, as soon as he stepped into the back yard, Miksha knew the animal was in the trap: the stench carried as far as the gate. Reb Mendel, however, was nowhere in sight. Worn out by his long vigils, he had yielded to sleep and to fate. With his heavy peasant hand, Miksha patted Reb Mendel's one remaining hen, which was petrified with fear, and let it into the back yard. Then he raised the lid, which had teeth of bent nails, and in the split second the animal's moist muzzle appeared through the crack, he slammed the lid down with his fist. No less skillfully, he pushed a rusty wire through the skunk's nostrils, tied its paws, and hung the animal on the doorpost. An awful stench. He made one slit around the neck, like a crimson necklace, then two more at the base of the paws. Peeling back the skin around the neck, he made two more slits, like buttonholes, for his fingers.

Awakened by the terrifying shrieks of the animal or by a nightmare, Reb Mendel suddenly appeared. Holding his nose with the skirt of his wrinkled caftan, he stared with bloodshot, horrified eyes at the live, bloody ball suspended on a wire and writhing on the doorpost. After wiping his knife on the grass, Miksha stood up and said, "Reb Mendel, I have released you from skunks once and for all." When Reb Mendel finally spoke, his voice sounded hoarse and terrible, like the voice of a prophet: "Wash the blood off your hands and face. And be damned, Herr Micksat!"

THE CONSEQUENCES

Miksha soon experienced on his own hide the meaning of Reb Mendel's curse, for the master craftsmen of the entire district of Antonovka sought recommendations for their apprentices from no one but Reb Mendel. At the mention of Miksha's name, the Jew would rave in Yiddish and Hebrew alternately, beating his breast and pulling his hair as if someone had mentioned a dybbuk. Not even Reb Jusef, the worst craftsman, and not only among tailors, would keep him. Learning of Reb Mendel's curse, he fired Miksha after only two days. In return, Miksha solemnly swore that one day he would revenge himself for the injury the Talmudists had inflicted on him.

AIMICKE

The same year, Miksha became acquainted with a certain Aimicke, E. V. Aimicke, who introduced himself as a law student. This Aimicke had previously worked for the Digtaryev firm as a warehouse foreman, but he had been fired, or so he claimed, because of his illegal activities. Miksha and Aimicke, united by the same hate, tried to earn their livelihood by helping out in the hunts Count Bagaryan organized in the neighboring countryside, in which Antonovka's lumpen-proletariat served as a substitute for dogs. Sitting in the heavy shade of elm trees, listening to the distant call of hunting horns and the nervous barking of hounds, Aimicke talked to Miksha about a future without hounds, nobility, and hunting horns. When the triumphant call was sounded, Miksha barely had time to run to the place where the blood of the wild boar was flowing, and where the nobility, accompanied by the hellish yelping of the dogs, toasted one another, using curved, silver-rimmed horns, which had to be emptied at a single draught. At a secret meeting in the cellar of a house in the suburb of Antonovka, that same Aimicke (who after two months was working again in the warehouse of the Digtaryev firm) accepted Miksha into his organization. At the same time, he demanded that Miksha find work again, lest the revolutionary blade in him become dull.

Luck was with Miksha. One August afternoon, while he was lying at the edge of a ditch near the post road bordering Antonovka, Herr Baltescu passed by in his carriage. "Is it true," he asked, "that you flayed a live skunk and turned his skin inside out like a glove?" "It's true," answered Miksha; "although it's none of your business, Herr Baltescu." "Starting tomorrow you can work for me," said Herr Baltescu, not at all ruffled by Miksha's arrogance. "But you should know," he shouted to him, "my lambs are Astrakhan." "Anyone who can flay a live skunk knows how to turn an Astrakhan's skin inside out without making a slit for the thumbs," Miksha shouted after him self-confidently.

THE ASSIGNMENT

At the end of September, Miksha was returning on his bicycle from the estate of Herr Baltescu, the fur merchant of Antonovka. Over the forest rose a red cloud, anticipating the autumn winds. Along the way Aimicke, on his own shiny bicycle, joined him, and for a while rode alongside without saying a word. Then he set up a meeting with Miksha for the following evening, and abruptly turned into a side street. Miksha arrived at the appointed hour and gave the agreed-upon signal. Aimicke opened the door but did not turn on the light. "I'll be brief," he said. "I set up a meeting with each of the members at a different time and place. The police agents showed up at only one of these places." He paused. "At Bagaryan's mill," he finally said. Miksha was silent. He waited to hear the traitor's name. "You don't ask," said Aimicke, "who I was going to meet at Bagaryan's mill."

"Whoever it is," said Miksha laconically, "I wouldn't like to be in his skin."

Aimicke didn't tell him the name of the traitor that night. He never told him, as if he didn't want that dishonored name to pass his lips. He told him only that he was relying on his loyalty and hatred. And he said: "You'll see the face of the traitor. But don't get taken in by appearances: a traitor's face can take on a look of great righteousness."

Miksha spent a sleepless night. He tried to slip the deadly mask of the traitor onto the face of each of his comrades, but while it fitted the face of each, it suited none completely. Wearing a rubber apron, bloody to his elbows, he spent the entire next day slaughtering and skinning lambs on Herr Baltescu's estate. At dusk he washed himself at the water trough, put on his dark suit, tucked a red carnation in the brim of his hat, and rode to the edge of the forest on his bicycle. He continued to the mill on foot, through the autumn forest, treading the thick leaves, which muffled the terrible resolution of his footsteps.

THE FACE OF THE TRAITOR

Leaning on the rusty fence by the millrace, staring at the muddy whirlpools, Hanna Krzyzewska was waiting for him. There beside Bagaryan's abandoned and rotting mill, watching the water carrying the yellow leaves, she might have been thinking about the somber passing of the seasons. She had freckles on her face (just barely visible now in the twilight of the autumn evening), but they didn't have to be a mark of Cain, those sunspots—maybe a mark of race and the curse, but not a mark of betrayal. She had arrived in Antonovka about a month ago, after fleeing Poland, where the

police were after her. Before she reached the border, she had
spent five hours in the icy cold of a railroad water tank,
fortifying her spirit with verses of Bronyewski. The comrades
had made her a set of false papers, after checking on her
past: her record was impeccable (except for the tiny blemish
of her bourgeois background). In Munkachev she had given
German lessons, with a strong Yiddish accent, served as a
link between the Munkachev and Antonovka cells, and read
Klara Zetkin and Lafargue.

THE EXECUTION OF THE ASSIGNMENT

Following Aimicke's example, Miksha didn't say a word. To
tell the truth, he had more right to do this than Aimicke,
because he had seen the Face of the Traitor. Did he think at
that moment that over the face of Hanna Krzyzewska—the
face sprinkled with freckles like sand—the mask of a traitor
clung like a golden death mask? The documents we use
speak the terrible language of facts, and in them the word
"soul" has the sound of sacrilege. But what can be established
with certainty is the following: in the role of executor of
justice, Miksha, without a word, put his short fingers around
the girl's neck and tightened them until the body of Hanna
Krzyzewska went limp. The executor of the assignment
paused for a moment. By the terrible rules of the crime, the
corpse should be disposed of. Bending over the girl, he
looked around (only the threatening shadows of the trees
everywhere), took hold of her legs, and dragged her to the
river. What happened after that, from the moment he pushed
the body into the water, was like an ancient tale in which
justice must triumph and death uses various tricks to avoid
the sacrifice of children and maidens. Miksha saw, in the
middle of the concentric circles, the body of the drowned

girl and heard her frantic cries. It was no illusion, no phantom that lurked in the bad conscience of murderers. It was
Hanna Krzyzewska, cutting through the icy water with
panicky but sure strokes, freeing herself from the heavy
sheepskin jacket with two red lilies stitched at the waist. The
murderer (who shouldn't be called that yet) stared aghast
at the girl advancing toward the other bank, and at the
sheepskin jacket borne by the fast current of the river. The
uncertainty lasted only seconds. Running downstream, Miksha crossed the trestle and reached the other side as the howl
of a steam engine and the humming of the rails announced
a train's arrival from afar. The girl lay in the mire by the
bank among the knobby stalks of water willows. Breathing
heavily, she tried to straighten up, but no longer to escape.
As he plunged his short Bukovina knife with the rosewood
handle into her breast, Miksha, sweaty and gasping, could
barely make out a word or two from the quivering, muffled,
choking onrush of syllables that reached him through the
slush, blood, and screams. His stabs were quick now, inflicted with a self-righteous hate which gave his arm impetus.
Through the clacking of the train wheels and the muffled
thunder of the iron trestle, the girl began, before the death
rattle, to speak—in Romanian, in Polish, in Ukrainian, in
Yiddish, as if her death were only the consequence of some
great and fatal misunderstanding rooted in the Babylonian
confusion of languages.

Illusions do not play games with those who have seen
a dead body arise. Miksha took the entrails out of the corpse
to prevent it from rising to the surface, then shoved it into the
water.

THE UNIDENTIFIED BODY

The corpse was discovered a week later, some seven miles downstream from the scene of the crime. The notice given by the Czech police in the *Police Gazette,* describing a drowned woman with good teeth and reddish-brown hair, between eighteen and twenty years of age, elicited no response. So the victim's identity was not established, despite the efforts of the police of the three neighboring countries to solve the mystery. Since this was an uneasy time of mutual suspicion and espionage, such interest in this case is easily understood. Unlike the daily papers, which also carried the news about the drowned woman, the *Police Gazette* gave a detailed description of the wounds that caused the death. It cited all the injuries in the areas of the chest, neck, and back, enumerating twenty-seven stabs inflicted with "a sharp object, most likely a knife." One of the articles described the way in which the body had been relieved of its abdominal organs, whence the likelihood that the perpetrator of the crime was an individual with "indubitable knowledge of anatomy." Despite certain doubts, the circumstances suggested a sex crime, and as such, after a futile six-month investigation, it was placed *ad acta.*

THE MYSTERIOUS CONNECTIONS

Toward the end of November 1934, the police of Antonovka arrested a certain Aimicke, E. V. Aimicke, who was suspected of setting fire to the warehouse of the Digtaryev firm. This incident touched off a chain of puzzling and mysterious connections. At the moment the fire started, Aimicke had gone to take refuge in the neighboring village tavern, to which the clear loops of his bicycle tracks in the thick autumn mud, like Ariadne's thread, brought the police. They took the frightened Aimicke away. Then came a fantastic and unexpected confession: he had been informing the police about the secret political meetings held in the cellar of the house at No. 5 Yephimovska Street. Along with a great many confusing and contradictory motives for his action, he stated his sympathy with the anarchists. The police did not believe him. Having endured another few days in solitary confinement, and broken down by interrogation, Aimicke mentioned the case of the murdered girl. This was to be the key evidence in his behalf: since the members of the cell had definite reasons to suspect that someone among them was an informer, he had to sacrifice one of the members. Hanna Krzyzewska, who had joined the organization recently, was for many reasons the most suitable one to be denounced as a traitor. Then he gave a detailed description of the girl and the manner of her execution, as well as the name of the killer.*

THE CONFESSION

When Czechoslovakia and the Soviet Union signed a treaty of mutual aid, thereby putting aside for the time being the always sensitive question of borders, wide horizons of mutual cooperation opened up to the police of both countries. The

---

* Aimicke took the secret of his action to his grave: on the night following his confession, he allegedly hanged himself in his cell under unusual circumstances, which led to the justified suspicion that he had been murdered. Some investigators maintained that Aimicke was a German spy and provocateur who broke down; according to others, he was only a police informer whom the police eliminated as a dangerous witness. The hypothesis offered by Gul, that Aimicke lost his head over the beautiful Polish girl, who wouldn't yield to him, should not be dismissed.

Czech police handed over the names of several Sudeten Germans, proven spies of the Reich, while in return the Soviets gave them information about some former Czech citizens of no great importance to Soviet Intelligence and others who could not justify their flight into the Soviet Union on ideological grounds. Among the latter was a certain Micksat Hantesku, called Miksha. Since the Czech police thought him to be a murderer (the connection between the murdered girl, the disappearance of Hantesku, and Aimicke's statement was not difficult to make), they asked that he be handed over. Only then did Soviet Intelligence pay attention to the citizen M. L. Hanteshy, who worked on the state farm Red Freedom, where he was an excellent slaughterhouse worker. He was arrested in November 1936. After nine months of solitary confinement and dreadful torture, during which almost all his teeth were knocked out and his collarbone broken, Miksha finally asked to see the interrogator. They gave him a chair, a sheet of coarse paper, and a pencil. They told him: "Write, and stop making demands!" Miksha confessed, in black and white, that over two years ago, as a duty to the Party, he had killed the traitor and provocateur Hanna Krzyzewska, but he resolutely denied having raped her. While he wrote out the confession in his rough peasant hand, he was observed, from the wall of the modest interrogator's office, by the portrait of the One Who Must Be Believed. Miksha looked up at that portrait, at that good-natured, smiling face, the kind face of a wise old man, so much like his grandfather's; he looked up at him pleadingly, and with reverence. After months of starvation, beating, and torture, this was a bright moment in Miksha's life, this warm and pleasant interrogator's office, where an old Russian stove crackled as one had long ago in Miksha's house in Bukovina, this tranquillity beyond the muffled blows and the shrieks of prisoners, this portrait that smiled at him so like a father. In a sudden rapture of faith, Miksha wrote down his confession: that he was an agent of the Gestapo, that he had worked to sabotage the Soviet government. At the same time he cited twelve accomplices in the great conspiracy. They were: I. V. Torbukov, an engineer; I. K. Goldman, a supervisor of operations at a chemical factory in Kamerov; A. K. Berlicky, a surveyor and Party secretary of a state farm; M. V. Korelin, a district judge; F. M. Olshevsky, the president of the Krasnoyarsk collective farm; S. I. Solovyeva, a teacher of history; E. V. Kvapilova, a professor; M. M. Nehavkim, a priest; D. M. Dogatkin, a physicist; J. K. Maresku, a typesetter; E. M. Mendel, a master tailor; and M. L. Jusef, a tailor.

Each of them received twenty years. At dawn on May 18, 1938, in the Butirek prison yard, with the noise of running tractors in the background, the alleged leader and organizer of the conspiracy, A. K. Berlicky, was shot, along with twenty-nine members of another conspiracy.

Micksat Hantesku died of pellagra in Ezvestkovo Prison Camp on New Year's Eve, 1941.

THE SOW THAT EATS HER FARROW

FOR BORISLAV PEKIĆ

THE LAND OF ETERNITY

The first act of the tragedy, or comedy (in the scholastic sense of the word), whose main character is a certain Gould Verschoyle, begins as all earthly tragedies do: with birth. The rejected positivist formula of milieu and race can be applied to human beings to the same degree as to Flemish art. Thus the first act of the tragedy begins in Ireland, "the ultima Thule, the land on the other side of knowledge," as one of Dedalus's doubles calls it; in Ireland, "the land of sadness, hunger, despair, and violence," according to another explorer, who is less inclined to myth and more to laborious earthy prose. However, in him too a certain lyrical quality is not in harmony with the cruelty of the region:"The ultimate step of the sunset, Ireland is the last land to see the fading of the day. Night has already fallen on Europe while the slanting rays of the sun still purple the fjords and wastelands in the West. But let the dark clouds form, let a star fall, and suddenly the island again becomes as in a legend, that distant place covered with fog and darkness, which for so long marked the boundary of the known world to navigators. And on the other side is a break: the dark sea in which the dead once found their land of eternity. Their black ships on shores with strange names testify to a time when travel had something metaphysical about it: they summon up dreams without shores, without return."

THE ECCENTRICS

Dublin is a city that breeds a menagerie of eccentrics, the most notorious in the whole Western world: nobly disappointed, aggressive bohemians, professors in redingotes, superfluous prostitutes, infamous drunkards, tattered prophets, fanatical revolutionaries, sick nationalists, flaming anarchists, widows decked out in combs and jewelry, hooded priests. All day long this carnivalesque cohort parades along the Liffey. In the absence of more reliable sources, Bourniquel's picture of Dublin enables us to get a sense of the experience Gould Verschoyle would inevitably take with him from the island, an experience that is drawn into the soul just as the terrible stench of fish meal from the cannery near the harbor is drawn into the lungs.

With a certain rash anticipation, we would be inclined to view this carnivalesque cohort as the last image our hero would see in a rapid succession of images: the noble menagerie of Irish eccentrics (to which, in some ways, he also belonged) descending along the Liffey all the way down to the anchorage, and disappearing as if into hell.

THE BLACK MARSH

Gould Verschoyle was born in one such suburb of Dublin within reach of the harbor, where he listened to ships' whistles, that piercing howl which tells the righteous young heart that there are worlds and nations outside "Dubh-linn," this black marsh in which the stench and injustice are more heavily oppressive than anywhere else. Following the example of his father—who rose from bribe-taking customs official to even more wretched (in the moral sense) bureaucrat, and from passionate Parnellite to bootlicker and puritan—Gould Verschoyle acquired a revulsion for his native land, which is only one of the guises of perverted and masochistic patriotism. "The cracked looking glass of a servant, the sow that ears her farrow"—at nineteen Verschoyle wrote this cruel sentence, which referred more to Ireland than to his parents.

Wearied by the vain prattle in dark pubs where conspiracies and assassinations were plotted by phony priests, poets, and traitors, Gould Verschoyle wrote in his journal the sentence spoken by a certain tall nearsighted student, without foreseeing the tragic consequence that these words would have: "Anyone with any self-respect cannot bear to remain in Ireland and must go into exile, fleeing the country struck by the wrathful hand of Jupiter."

This was written in the entry for May 19, 1935.

In August of the same year he boarded a merchant ship, the *Ringsend*, which was sailing for Morocco. After a three-day stopover in Marseilles, the *Ringsend* sailed without one of its crew; or, to be exact, the place of the radio operator Verschoyle was filled by a newcomer. In February 1936 we find Gould Verschoyle near Guadalajara in the 15th Anglo-

American Brigade bearing the name of the legendary Lincoln. Verschoyle was then twenty-eight years old.

FADED PHOTOGRAPHS

Here the reliability of the documents, resembling, as they do, palimpsests, is suspended for a moment. The life of Gould Verschoyle blends and merges with the life and death of the young Spanish Republic. We have only two snapshots. One, with an unknown soldier next to the ruins of a shrine. On the back, in Verschoyle's handwriting: "Alcázar. Viva la República." His high forehead is half covered by a Basque beret, a smile hovers around his lips, on which one can read (from today's perspective) the triumph of the victor and the bitterness of the defeated: the paradoxical reflections that, like a line on the forehead, foreshadow inevitable death. Also, a group snapshot with the date November 5, 1936. The picture is blurred. Verschoyle is in the second row, still with a Basque beret pulled over his forehead. In front of the lined-up group a landscape stretches out, and it would not be hard to believe that we are in a cemetery. Is this the Honor Guard that fired salvos into the sky or into living flesh? The face of Gould Verschoyle jealously guards this secret. Over the rows of soldiers' heads, in the distant blue an airplane hovers like a crucifix.

CAUTIOUS SPECULATIONS

I see Verschoyle retreating from Málaga on foot, in the leather coat he took from a dead Falangist (under the coat there was only the thin, naked body and a silver cross on a leather string); I see him charging toward a bayonet, carried along by his own war cry as if by the wings of the exterminating angel; I see him in a shouting contest with Anarchists, whose black flag is raised on the bare hills near Guadalajara, and who are ready to die a noble, senseless death; I see him under the red-hot sky by a cemetery near Bilbao, listening to lectures in which, as at the Creation, life and death, heaven and earth, freedom and tyranny are fixed within boundaries; I see him discharging a clip of bullets into the air at planes, impotent, felled right afterward by fire, earth, and shrapnel; I see him shaking the dead body of the student Armand Joffroy, who died in his arms somewhere near Santander; I see him, his head wrapped in filthy bandages, lying in an improvised hospital near Gijón, listening to the ravings of the wounded, one of whom is calling on God in Irish; I see him talking with a young nurse who lulls him to sleep like a child, singing in a tongue unknown to him, and later he, half asleep and full of morphine, sees her climbing into the bed of a Pole who has had a leg amputated, and soon thereafter he hears, as in a nightmare, her aching love rattle; I see him somewhere in Catalonia, at the improvised battalion headquarters, sitting in front of the telegraph, repeating desperate calls for help while a radio in the nearby cemetery plays the gay and suicidal songs of the Anarchists; I see him suffering from conjunctivitis and diarrhea, and I see him naked to the waist, shaving by a well of poisoned water.

BETWEEN ACTS

In late May 1937, somewhere in the suburbs of Barcelona, Verschoyle requested to see the battalion commander. The commander, just past forty, looked like a well-preserved old man. Bent over his desk, he was signing death sentences. His aide, buttoned up to his neck and wearing shiny hunting boots, stood beside him and was pressing a blotter after each signature. The room was stuffy. The commander wiped his face with a batiste handkerchief. Rhythmical explosions of heavy-caliber grenades were heard in the distance. The commander motioned to Verschoyle to speak. "Coded messages are getting into the wrong hands," said Verschoyle. "Whose?" asked the commander somewhat absentmindedly. The Irishman hesitated, suspiciously glancing at the aide. The commander then adopted the vocabulary of Verdun: "Speak up, son. Into whose hands?" The Irishman was silent for a moment, then bent over the desk and whispered something into the commander's ear. The commander rose, approached Verschoyle, and accompanied him to the door, all the while patting him on the shoulder the way recruits and dreamers are patted. That was all.

A CALL FOR TRAVEL

Verschoyle spent the hellish night between May 31 and June 1 in front of the Morse telegraph, sending stern messages to the forward positions over toward the mountains of Almería. The night was muggy and illuminated by rockets, which made the region look unreal. Just before dawn Verschoyle handed the telegraph over to a young Basque. The Irishman walked ten paces into the woods and, exhausted, lay face down on the damp grass.

He was awakened by a messenger from headquarters. Verschoyle first glanced at the sky, then at his watch; he hadn't slept more than forty minutes. The messenger gave him an order in a tone unbefitting his rank: there was a ship in the harbor whose radio didn't work—it must be repaired; when the job was finished, a report should be submitted to the second-in-command; *Viva la República!* Verschoyle rushed into the tent, picked up the leather bag with his tools, and set off with the messenger to the harbor. During the night, someone had written a victorious slogan with white paint, still dripping, on the door of the customhouse: VIVA LA MUERTE. On the open sea far from the dock, a silhouette of a ship was outlined through the morning fog. The messenger and the sailors in the rowboat exchanged unnecessary passwords. Verschoyle got into the rowboat without looking back.

THE BRASS-PLATED DOOR

Charred timbers floated everywhere, remnants of a ship torpedoed during the night. Verschoyle watched the ashen sea, and this reminded him of scorned and scornworthy Ireland. (Even so, we cannot believe that there wasn't a touch of nostalgia in this scorn.) His traveling companions were silent, busy with their heavy oars. Soon they approached the ship, and Verschoyle noticed that they were being watched from the upper deck; the helmsman had handed a pair of binoculars to the captain.

Here follow some technical details, perhaps unimportant to the story. The ship was an old wooden steamer of some five hundred tons which was officially transporting anthracite to the French city of Rouen. Its brass parts—handholds, bolts, locks, and window frames—were almost green with tarnish, and the ship's flag, covered with coal soot, could hardly be identified.

Verschoyle climbed the ship's slippery rope ladder, accompanied by the two sailors from the rowboat (one of whom had relieved him of his leather bag, so the guest could climb more easily). There was no one on deck. The two sailors took him to a cabin below. The cabin was empty, and the door was plated with that same tarnished brass. Verschoyle heard the turning of the key in the lock. At the same time he real-ized—more in rage than terror—that he had fallen into a trap, naïvely, like a fool.

The journey lasted eight days. Verschoyle spent these eight days and nights below deck, in a narrow cabin by the engine room, where the deafening noise of engines crushed the current of his thought and his sleep like a millstone. In a strange reconciliation with his fate (very deceptive, as shall be seen), he didn't bang on the door, he didn't call for help. It seemed he didn't even think of escape, which in any case was useless. In the morning he would wash himself over the tin basin, then glance at the food (herring, salmon, black bread, which they gave him three times a day through the round opening in the door), and without touching anything but water, lie down again on the hard sailor's bunk. He would stare through the porthole at the monotonous waves of the open sea. On the third day Verschoyle awoke from a nightmare: on the narrow bench across from his bunk, two men sat silently watching him. Verschoyle abruptly stood up.

THE TRAVELING COMPANIONS

Blue-eyed, with healthy white teeth, the visitors smiled at Verschoyle amicably. With an unnatural politeness (un-natural for the time and place), they also rose at once, and introduced themselves, slightly nodding their heads. To Verschoyle, who introduced himself, the syllables of his own name suddenly sounded strange and altogether alien.

The next five days the three men spent in the hot, narrow cabin behind the brass-plated door in a terrible game of chance, resembling three-handed poker in which the loser pays with his life. Interrupting the discussion only to gobble a piece of dried herring (the fourth day Verschoyle also began to eat) or to refresh their dry throats and take a breather from their shouting (and then the deafening noise of the engines would become only the reverse of silence), the three men spoke of justice, of freedom, of the proletariat, of the goals of the Revolution, vehemently trying to prove their beliefs, as if they had purposely chosen this semidark cabin of a ship on international waters as the only possible objective and neutral terrain for this terrible game of argument, passion, persuasion, and fanaticism. With rolled-up sleeves, unshaven and sweaty, worn out from near fasting, they stopped the discussion completely only once: on the fifth day, the two visitors (besides their names, all that was known was that they were about twenty years old and not members of the crew) left Verschoyle alone for several hours. During that time, through the deafening noise of the engines, the Irishman heard the sound of a familiar foxtrot coming from the deck. Before midnight the music suddenly died, and the visitors returned, tipsy. They told Verschoyle that there was a celebration on board: a cablegram received that afternoon by the radioman had told them that their ship, the *Vitebsk,* had changed its name to *Ordzhonikidze.* They offered him some vodka. He refused, fearing poison. The young men understood and finished the vodka, laughing at the Irishman's distrust.

The sudden and unexpected halt of the engine noise abruptly interrupted the conversation in the cabin, as if that deadly rhythm was the ritual accompaniment which until then had given impetus and inspiration to their thoughts and arguments. Now they were silent, totally mute, listening to the waves splashing at the sides of the ship, to the thud of footsteps on deck, and the prolonged scraping of heavy chains. It was after midnight when the door of the cabin was unlocked, and the three men left their quarters strewn with cigarette butts and fishbones.

THE HANDCUFFS

The *Vitebsk-Ordzhonikidze* dropped anchor in the open sea nine miles from Leningrad. From the cluster of distant lights on the shore, one soon separated, and grew larger, while the wind, like an advance guard, brought the noise of the boat that was approaching the ship. Three men in uniform, one with the rank of captain and the other two without insignia, approached Verschoyle and aimed their guns at him. Verschoyle put his hands up. They searched him, then tied a rope around his waist. Verschoyle compliantly went down the rope ladder and into the motorboat, where they handcuffed him to the seat. He watched the ghostly silhouette of the ship illuminated by searchlights. He saw his two companions also coming down the ladder with ropes tied around their waists. Soon all three sat side by side, handcuffed to the seat.

THE JUST SENTENCE

The true outcome of the six-day battle of words and arguments waged by the Irishman Gould Verschoyle and his two traveling companions will probably remain a secret to the contemporary researcher. It will also remain a psychological secret, and legally a most interesting one, whether it is possible for a man cornered by fear and despair to so sharpen his arguments and experience that he is able—without external pressure, without the use of force and torture—to throw into doubt all that has been developed through many years of upbringing, lectures, habit, and training in the consciousness of two other men. Then, perhaps, the decision of the high tribunal, which, according to some loftier justice, had pronounced the same stern sentence (eight years of imprisonment) on each of the three participants in that long game of persuasion, might not seem entirely arbitrary. For even if it is believed that the two men succeeded, through dense and exhausting ideological polemics, in dispelling certain suspicions that had appeared in the head of the Republican Verschoyle (suspicions with possible far-reaching consequences), there was a perfectly justified suspicion that the other two had also felt the fatal influence of certain counterarguments: in the merciless battle of equal opponents, as in a bloody cockfight, no one comes out unharmed, regardless of which one walks away with the empty glory of victory.*

FINALE

We lose track of Verschoyle's two companions in Murmansk, on the banks of the Baltic Sea, where for a time during the terrible winter of 1942 they lay in the same section of the prison camp's outpatient ward, half blind and wasted with scurvy: all their teeth had fallen out, and they looked like old men.

Gould Verschoyle was murdered in November 1945, in Karaganda, after an unsuccessful attempt to escape. His

---

* During the interrogation Verschoyle stubbornly denied that, on that fatal day, during his report, he had whispered into the commander's ear that coded messages were reaching Moscow. He could not have known that the interrogator had before him the report of the second-in-command in which Verschoyle's words, expressing the dangerous and sacrilegious suspicion "that Soviet secret agents are trying to usurp the leadership positions in the Republican army," were repeated verbatim. A brief encounter with the second-in-command, Chelyustnikov, at the transit station in Karaganda revealed this secret to him: the commander had informed his aide of Verschoyle's confidential declaration as if it were a good joke.

frozen, naked corpse, bound with wire and hung upside down, was displayed in front of the camp's entrance as a warning to all those who dream of the impossible.

POSTSCRIPT

In the commemorative volume *Ireland to Spain,* published by the Federation of Dublin Veterans, the name of Gould Verschoyle is mistakenly entered among some one hundred Irish Republicans slain in the battle of Brunete. Thus Verschoyle enjoyed the bitter glory of being pronounced dead some eight years before his actual death. The famous battle of Brunete, waged bravely by the Lincoln Battalion, took place the night of July 8–9, 1938.

THE MECHANICAL LIONS

HOMMAGE À ANDRÉ GIDE

THE COLOSSUS

The only historical personage in this story, Édouard Herriot, the leader of the French Radical Socialists, Mayor of Lyons, member of the Chamber of Deputies, Premier, musicologist, etc., will perhaps not play the most important part. Not because (let us state at once) this part is of less importance to the story than that of the other person—unhistorical though no less real—who appears here, but simply because there are many other documents about historical personages. Let us not forget that Édouard Herriot himself was a writer and journalist,* and a very distinguished politician whose biography can be found in any decent encyclopedia.

One source gives the following description of Herriot: "Big, strong, broad-shouldered, with an angular head covered by thick, bristly hair, a face shaped as if by a pruning

---

* *Mme Récamier et ses amis, La Russie nouvelle, Pourquoi je suis radical socialiste, Lyons n'est plus, Fôret normande, Jadis, Souvenirs, Vie de Beethoven,* etc.

knife, and cut off by a short, thick mustache, this man gave
the impression of great strength. His voice, marvelous in
itself and adaptable to the subtlest nuances and most modu-
lated stresses, easily dominated any disorder. He knew how
to control his facial expression." The same source gives the
following description of his character: "It was a real spec-
tacle to see him on the podium, alternating between serious
and playful tones, between confidential and Jeremian procla-
mations of some principle. And if someone contradicted him,
he accepted the little provocation; while the other expounded
his views, a broad smile spread over Édouard Herriot's face—
the preliminary sign of a devastating remark, which, the moment it was spoken, provoked a riot of laughter and applause
to the utter confusion of the speaker caught in the trap. That
smile, it is true, would disappear if the criticism was voiced
in an insulting tone. Such attacks infuriated him and provoked in him a violent reaction, the more so since he was
always cautious—a sensitivity which many saw as vanity."*

THE OTHER ONE

Of the other important person in this story, A. L. Chelyustnikov, we know only that he was about forty, tall, a little
hunchbacked, blond, talkative, a boaster and womanizer and,
until recently, the editor of the Ukrainian paper *New Dawn*.
He was expert at poker and skat, and could play polkas and
chastushkas on the accordion. Other testimony about him is
highly contradictory and therefore perhaps unimportant. I am
including it, although some of the sources are rightly suspect:
he was a political commissar in the Spanish Civil War and
distinguished himself in the cavalry in the battles around

* André Ballit in *Le Monde*, March 28, 1957.

Barcelona; one night, despite a high malarial fever, he slept with two nurses; by trickery he brought an Irishman suspected of sabotage to the Soviet cargo ship *Ordzhonikidze,* under the pretext that the ship's radio had to be repaired; he actually knew Ordzhonikidze personally; for three years he was the lover of the wife of an extremely prominent person (and for precisely this reason was sent to a prison camp); in his school's amateur drama group in Voronezh, he played the role of Arcady in Ostrovsky's play *The Forest.*

Even if the cited documents exude a certain unreliability, especially the last few, one of Chelyustnikov's stories—the one relating to Herriot—although seemingly a figment of the imagination, nevertheless deserves to be recorded. I am doing so because one can hardly doubt its credibility, and because everything suggests that some of Chelyustnikov's stories, strange as they seem, are nevertheless based on real events. The most convincing proof of all is that the following story was in a way confirmed by Édouard Herriot himself, that dazzling intelligence (*"une intelligence rayonnante"*), as Daladier accurately described him. So I will tell the story of that encounter of long ago between Chelyustnikov and Herriot as well as I can, freeing myself for a moment of that awful burden of documents in which the story is buried, while referring the skeptical and curious reader to the appended bibliography, where he will find the necessary proof. (Perhaps it would have been wiser if I had chosen some other form of expression—an essay or a monograph—where I could use all these documents in the usual way. Two things, however, prevent me: the inappropriateness of citing actual oral testimony of reliable people as documentation; and my inability to forgo the pleasure of narration, which allows the author the deceptive idea that he is creating the world and thereby, as they say, changing it.)

THE TELEPHONE AND THE GUN

On that cold November night in 1934 Chelyustnikov, a contributing editor of the local newspaper responsible for cultural affairs and the fight against religion, was sleeping naked as a baby in a large aristocratic bed in a cozy room on the third floor of a house on Yegorovka Street. His shiny raspberry-colored boots were leaning neatly against the bed, while his clothes and underwear lay strewn about the room, mixed haphazardly (a sign of passionate haste) with a woman's silk underwear. The room gave off the warm smell of sweat, vodka, and cologne.

Chelyustnikov had a dream (if he is to be believed), in which he was to appear on stage in a role, probably as Arcady in *The Forest,* but he couldn't find his clothes anywhere. Terrified (in the dream), he heard the bell calling him to the stage, but he stood as if petrified, or, rather, sat, naked and hairy, unable to move. Suddenly, as if all this was happening onstage, the curtain rose, and through the dazzling side lights, which held him in the cross fire of their rays, he made out the audience, up in the balcony and down in the orchestra, their heads illuminated by purple haloes. In the first row, he thought he could recognize the members of the Provincial Committee, and among them he clearly distinguished the shiny bald spot of Comrade M., the editor-in-chief of *New Dawn,* who was choking with laughter and mocking and insulting him about his masculinity. The bell in the dressing room kept ringing, more loudly and insistently, so that Chelyustnikov thought (in the dream) that it was a fire alarm, that the curtains had caught fire, and that at any moment a general scrambling and panic would break out while he would stay there on the stage, naked as a baby, unable to move, exposed to the mercy of the flames. His right hand suddenly broke free of the spell, and, on the border between dream and reality, instinctively reached for the gun that, by force of habit, he kept under his pillow. He turned on the light on the night table, and knocked over a glass of vodka. At the same instant he realized that his boots were now more important than his gun, and quickly jumped into them, as into a saddle. The wife of the editor-in-chief of *New Dawn* turned in her sleep and then, awakened by the ringing, opened her beautiful, slightly puffy Asiatic eyes. To their relief, the telephone abruptly stopped ringing. There followed an anxious whispered conference. Nastasia Fedotevna M., confused and frightened, tried to put on her bra, which Chelyustnikov had tossed over to her from the pile of clothes. The phone started ringing again. "Get up," Chelyustnikov said, putting the gun under his belt. Nastasia Fedotevna stared at him, horrified. Chelyustnikov walked over to the flustered woman, placed a kiss between her ample breasts, and said: "Pick up the phone." The woman got up, and Chelyustnikov covered her gallantly with his leather coat. A moment later he heard her voice. "Who? Chelyustnikov?" (The man put his finger to his lips.) "I have no idea." (Pause.) Then the woman replaced the receiver, from which an abrupt click could be heard, and sank into the armchair. "The Provincial Committee..." (Pause.) "They say it's urgent."

THE FOLDER

Before he returned to his cold apartment on Sokolov Prospect, Chelyustnikov wandered awhile through the snowy streets. He used a roundabout route along the Dnieper, and it took him a whole hour to get home. He slipped off his leather coat, poured himself a glass of vodka, and turned on the radio. Scarcely five minutes had passed when the telephone rang. He let it ring three times before picking up the receiver. He acted as if surprised by this late call (it was already past two), then said that, since it was urgent, he'd be there in half an hour at most: he had to put his clothes on, since he had just undressed. All right, they said, since it was urgent, they'd send the car to pick him up. Comrade Pyasnikov would explain everything to him in person.

Comrade Pyasnikov, secretary of the Provincial Committee, quickly came to the point: this morning around eleven o'clock Citizen Édouard Herriot, the leader of the French workers, would arrive in Kiev. Chelyustnikov replied that he had read in the paper of Herriot's visit to Moscow, but didn't know that he would visit Kiev also. Pyasnikov asked him if he realized how important the visit of such a man was. Chelyustnikov said, yes, he knew (although it wasn't too clear to him why this visit was so important or what part he was to play in it). As if he had sensed Chelyustnikov's uncertainty, Pyasnikov began to explain: Citizen Herriot, in spite of his political persuasion, entertained certain typical bourgeois suspicions of our revolutionary movement. He cited many details from the life and works of Herriot, emphasizing his petty bourgeois origins, citing his various positions, recounting his love for classical music and progressive movements the world over, and stressing the role he played in getting the land of the Bolsheviks (that was what he said, "the land of the Bolsheviks") recognized by France. Finally, Pyasnikov took a folder out of his desk drawer and started to leaf through it. "Here," he said, "for example, I quote: 'It is impossible even for an irreligious Frenchman' (as you can see, Herriot liberated himself from religious scruples, if one can believe him) 'even for an irreligious Frenchman not to raise his voice against the persecution of priests...' " (Here Comrade Pyasnikov paused, looking up at Chelyustnikov: "You understand?" Chelyustnikov nodded and Pyasnikov added: "For them, priests are still some kind of sacred cow, as they are for our peasants...of former times, of course.") " '...since that also represents an attack on freedom of thought. An attack which, after all, is totally unnecessary, et cetera, et cetera,' " said Pyasnikov closing the folder. "I think it's clear now?" "Yes," said Chelyustnikov, pouring himself a glass of water. He stayed in Comrade Pyasnikov's office until four in the morning. And he was on his feet again at seven. He had exactly four hours until the arrival of the train.

THE HOURS AND THE MINUTES

That important morning in the life of A. L. Chelyustnikov unfolded, hour by hour, as follows: at 7:00 he was awakened by the telephone service. He gulped down a glass of vodka on an empty stomach and, naked to the waist, washed himself with cold water. He dressed, shined his boots. For breakfast he scrambled a couple of eggs on the hot plate and ate them with cucumbers. At 7:20 he telephoned the Provincial Committee. Comrade Pyasnikov answered with his mouth full, apologizing: he hadn't left the office all night, he had dozed off sitting at the desk; he asked Chelyustnikov how he was; he had set up an appointment for him with Avram Romanich, a make-up man, in the lobby of the theater (the stage entrance) for four that afternoon; he should be prompt. At 7:25 Chelyustnikov phoned Nastasia Fedotevna. After a long pause (downstairs, the car sent by the Provincial Committee was honking) he heard the flustered voice of the wife of the editor-in-chief of New Dawn. She couldn't imagine why they had looked for him at her place last night. She was desperate.

If M. (her husband) found out, she'd poison herself. She wouldn't be able to stand the shame. Yes, yes, poison; rat poison. Through the torrent of her words, her babbling and sobbing, Chelyustnikov was hardly able to inject a word of comfort: she shouldn't worry, it was all pure coincidence, he'd explain everything, but not now, he was in a hurry, the car was waiting downstairs. And she shouldn't think of rat poison. At 7:30 he got into the black limousine parked in front of the house; a few minutes before 7:45 he arrived at the Provincial Committee. Comrade Pyasnikov's eyes were red and puffy. They downed a glass of vodka, talked things over, and made telephone calls from 8:00 to 9:30, using two different offices so as not to disturb each other. At 9:30 Comrade Pyasnikov, whose eyes were like a rabbit's, pushed a button on his large walnut desk, and the cleaning woman brought in tea. For a long time they sipped the hot tea, smiling at each other like those who have accomplished a difficult and important task. At 10:00 they left for the railroad station to check on the security. Comrade Pyasnikov demanded that the poster with the slogan RELIGION IS THE OPIATE OF THE PEOPLE be removed and promptly replaced by another with a somewhat more metaphysical sound: LONG LIVE THE SUN, DOWN WITH THE NIGHT. Exactly at 11:00, as the train carrying the highly important guest pulled into the station, Chelyustnikov detached himself from the welcoming committee and joined the security agents, who were standing to one side, dressed in civilian clothes. They were carrying suitcases and pretending to be casual, curious passengers welcoming the friendly visitor from France with spontaneous applause. Quickly sizing up Herriot (who seemed to be somehow insignificant, perhaps because of his beret), Chelyustnikov left through the side door, got into the car, and drove off.

He arrived at Saint Sophia at exactly 12:00.

THE PAST

The Cathedral of Saint Sophia was built as a murky tribute to the glorious days of Vladimir, Yaroslav, and Izyaslav. It is only a distant replica of the Korsun Monastery, named after the "holy city" of Kerson, or Korsun. The chronicles of the learned Nestor note that Prince Vladimir brought icons, church statuary, as well as "four bronze horses" from Korsun, the city of his baptism.* But since the first cornerstone of Saint Sophia was laid by the eternally blessed Vladimir, much water and blood and many corpses have flowed down the glorious Dnieper. The ancient Slavic gods continued to struggle for a long time against the celebrated caprice of the prince of Kiev who adopted the monotheistic faith of Christianity, and the pagan Russian people fought with pagan brutality against "the sons of Dazh-Bog," and for a long time cast their deadly arrows and spears on the winds, "the children of Stribog." The brutality of the believers in the true faith, however, was not less barbaric than pagan brutality, and the fanaticism of the believers in the tyranny of one god was still more fierce and efficient.

Holy Kiev, the mother of Russian cities, had some four hundred churches at the beginning of the eleventh century, and according to the chronicles of Dietmar of Merseburg, it became "the loveliest pearl of Byzantium and a rival of

---

* "Four bronze horses" (*chetire kone mediani*), some experts claim, should be rendered "four bronze icons" (*chetire ikone mediani*). In this lexical ambivalence, we can see primarily an example of the conflict and merging of the two idolatries: the pagan and the Christian. My source, Jean Descatte, discovered that all the pages relating to the Cathedral of Saint Sophia were taken almost verbatim from a French study of Russian art. He published an article on the subject in the *Journal de Police,* which is read in Bordeaux and Toulouse; like a distant echo this added another circle to the metaphysical message of the story "Dogs and Books."

Constantinople." Choosing the Byzantine Empire and faith, through Orthodoxy, Russia attached herself to an ancient and refined civilization, but because of its schism and the renunciation of Roman authority she was left to the mercy of the Mongol conquerers and could not rely on the protection of Europe. This schism, in turn, brought about the isolation of Russian Orthodoxy from the West; their churches were built on the sweat and bones of the peasants, ignorant of the high sweep of Gothic spires, while in the domain of sensibility Russia was never swept up by chivalry and would "beat her women as if the cult of the Lady never existed."

All this is more or less written on the walls and in the frescoes of Kiev's Saint Sophia. The rest is only historical data of lesser significance: the church was founded by Yaroslav the Wise in 1037, in eternal memory of the day he triumphed over the pagan Petchenegs. He ordered the magnificent Golden Door built near the portal of the church, so that the mother of Russian cities, Kiev, would not envy Constantinople. Its glory was short-lived. The Mongol hordes poured out of the steppes (1240), and leveled the holy city. But Saint Sophia was already in ruins: in 1240 her vaults collapsed. At the same time, the vaults of a church named Desatna also collapsed, killing hundreds of people who had taken refuge there to avoid brutal massacre by the Mongols. In his *Description of the Ukraine,* published in Rouen in 1651, the Master of Beauplan, a Norman nobleman in the service of the Polish king, wrote words that resemble an epitaph: "Of all the Kiev churches, only two remain as a memory to posterity. The rest are sad ruins: *reliquiae reliquiarum.*"

The most famous mosaic of Saint Sophia, "The Virgin Mother Blessing," was glorified by the people of Kiev under the name *Nerushimaya stena,* the indestructible wall—a distant allusion to the twelfth stanza of the Akatist Hymn.

Legend, however, justifies this name in another way: when the church collapsed, all its walls crumbled except those of the apse, which stood undamaged, a gift of the Virgin Mother in the mosaic.

A CIRCUS IN THE HOUSE OF GOD

As irrelevant as it may seem at first (we shall see, though, that this irrelevancy is only an illusion), we cannot fail to mention at this point those strange frescoes that decorate the walls of the circular staircases leading to the upper floor, where the princes and their guests, the boyars, could participate in the service without leaving the palace. These frescoes were found under painting done in 1843; due to haste and curiosity—the mother of invention as well as error—the restoration had been carried out with the utmost carelessness: to the old patina, to the shimmer of gold and vestments, the *nouveau riche* dazzle of boyar wealth and luxury was added. Other than that, the scenes were left untouched: under the azure firmament of Byzantium, the hippodrome and circus; at the focal point, the honorary loge of the Emperor and Empress, surrounded by their retinue; behind the barrier, grooms waiting to release their rearing horses into the arena; hard-faced warriors armed with spears, accompanied by a pack of hounds pursuing wild beasts; acrobats and actors performing their skills on the stage under the open sky; a muscular athlete holding a long pole on which an acrobat is climbing, as agile as a monkey; a gladiator armed with an ax, lunging at the tamet, who is wearing a bear's head.

The book of Constantine Porphyrogenitus, who speaks of the ceremonies at the Byzantine court in a chapter entitled "The Gothic Games," gives us the meaning of the above depiction: "The entertainments, called Ludus Gothicus, are held

every eighth day after Christmas at the will of His Gracious
Majesty, and during that time the guests of His Gracious
Majesty disguise themselves as Goths, wearing the masks and
heads of various cruel beasts."

So much for the past.

THE BREWERY

At present, Kiev's Saint Sophia shelters under its high vaults
a part of the Spartacus Brewery—the drying kiln and the
warehouse. The enormous twenty-ton tanks, set on stands
made of planks, run along the walls, and large, heavy steel
vats are scattered among the columns as far as the apse itself.
The drying kiln takes up two floors, with wooden gratings
reaching from the top of the windows to the arcades. (The
constant temperature of 50° Fahrenheit is particularly suitable for the growth of those useful bacteria that give beer its
unique taste.) Curved aluminum pipes pass through one of
the side windows, which has been removed, and connect the
drying kiln and tanks with the fermentation tank, which is
located in a large low building some hundred yards from the
church. Scaffolding and ladders connect the gratings, pipes,
and tanks, and the sour smell of hops and malt brings to the
ancient walls the scent of the boundless steppes after the
rain. The frescoes and altar are covered (as a result of a
recent decree) with long hemp curtains, which are draped
along the walls like gray flags. In the place where the Im-
maculate Virgin, "surprised by the sudden appearance of the
Archangel," once stood (or, more exactly, still stands under
the gray veil), there hangs the portrait of the Father of the
People in a heavy gilded frame: the work of the academic
painter Sokolov, a worthy artist. In a snowstorm an old
woman makes her way through the crowd, trying to kiss the

hand of the Gracious One, to kiss it like a peasant—sincerely. He smiles at the old woman, resting his hand on her shoulder, like a father. Soldiers, workers, and children watch with admiring eyes. Under the portrait, on the same wall, where through the folds of hemp the murky light from the two windows penetrates, stand billboards and graphs. Groggy and stupefied from the smell of hops, Chelyustnikov looked at the production graph as if, feverish, he were watching his own temperature chart.

ANOTHER RESTORATION

I. V. Braginsky, "participant in the Revolution, son of peasants, Bolshevik," chief production engineer, took off his cap, scratched his head, turned the paper over in his hands, and, probably for the third time, read it without comment. Meanwhile Chelyustnikov examined the interior of the church, looked up toward the high vaults, poked behind the scaffolding, estimated the weight of the tanks and vats, soundlessly moving his dry lips as he calculated. These high frescoed vaults reminded him of a small wooden church in his native village where long ago he had attended the service with his parents and listened to the mumbling of the priests and the singing of the congregation: a distant and unreal memory, which had faded away in him, a new man with a new outlook on life. The rest of what happened that day in Saint Sophia we learn from Chelyustnikov's own testimony: "Ivan Vasilevich, participant in the Revolution, son of peasants, Bolshevik, wasted two hours of our valuable time in useless prattle and persuasion. Believing the attainment of the monthly beer production quota to be more important than religious spectacles, he crumpled the People's Committee's order and threw it in my face. Aware that time was passing, I tried to reason with him, to explain that it was for the common good that the church be made ready for a religious service. Powerless against his stubbornness, I took him to the office and in private confided the secret to him, without mentioning the name of the visitor. Even this argument didn't convince him, nor did the several telephone calls I made from the military telephone in his quarters to the officials in charge. Finally I pulled out my last argument: I pointed my pistol at him.... Under my personal supervision a hundred and twenty prisoners from the nearby regional prison camp carried out another restoration of the church, in less than four hours. We leaned a part of the kiln against the wall and camouflaged it with hemp coverings and canvas, which we also threw over the scaffolding, as if the east wall were undergoing a real restoration. We removed the steel tanks and vats by rolling them on logs (by manpower alone, without technology) into the yard of the building containing the fermentation tank. At 3:45 I got into the car, and exactly at the appointed time reached the lobby of the theater, where Avram Romanich was waiting for me."

THE BEARD AND THE PRIEST'S HAT

We further cite Chelyustnikov's testimony: "Comrade Pyasnikov explained everything to him (to Avram Romanich) and, as he told me later, even made him sign a declaration promising to keep silent about the matter, as if it were a state secret. This obviously had its effect; Avram Romanich's hands trembled while he was fixing my beard. We borrowed the priest's robe from the theater wardrobe, with its purple sash, and the high priest's hat, and in a note to the management we stated that we needed these items for members of the culture brigade, who were launching antireligious shows in the villages and workers' collectives. Avram Romanich asked no more questions, and threw himself completely into his work; his hands soon stopped shaking. He was unquestionably good in his profession. Not only did he make me into a real archpriest, but on his own initiative he also gave me a fake paunch. 'When have you ever seen a thin priest, Citizen Chelyustnikov?' I agreed with this, and regardless of what later happened to him (which I won't dwell on here), I insist that Avram Romanich deserves almost as much credit for the success of the whole affair as I do: he gave me some advice that was of great value to me despite the fact that I had some stage experience. 'Citizen Chelyustnikov,' he said, now totally forgetting his fear and completely immersed in his work, 'don't forget for a moment that a beard, especially this kind of beard, is not held up by the head but by the chest. So right now, no time to lose, you must learn to coordinate the movement of your head and body.' He even gave me some useful advice about the service and the chanting—training he had probably acquired in the theater. (Or maybe in a synagogue; who the hell knows?) 'When you don't know what to say next, Citizen Chelyustnikov, keep mumbling in a low voice. Mumble as much as you can, as if you were angry with the congregation. And roll your eyes as if cursing the god you serve, even if just temporarily. As for chanting...' 'We haven't got time for that now,' I said. 'We'll chant later, Avram Romanich!' "

THE RASPBERRY-COLORED BOOTS

Chelyustnikov stayed in the dressing room a little over an hour—a relatively short time, considering the transformation he underwent. A. T. Kashalov, simply called Alyosha, the chauffeur of the Provincial Committee, who had driven him there, kissed his hand when he got in the car. "It was like a dress rehearsal," writes Chelyustnikov, "and I lost the stage fright I had felt when left without the coaching of Avram Romanich. At first I thought that Alyosha was kidding, but I soon realized that there was no limit to human credulity: if I had appeared with a crown on my head, he would probably have fallen on his knees in the mud and snow. It will take a great deal of time and effort," adds Chelyustnikov, not without bitterness and self-righteousness, "before all traces of the dark past are weeded out of the peasants' souls."

(Let us say at once: A. T. Kashalov never once admitted during the long interrogation, not even under the worst torture, that he had been made a fool of that day. When confronted with Chelyustnikov in the investigator's office, less than a month after the event, he obstinately maintained that he was only joking with Citizen Chelyustnikov. Despite his physical exhaustion, despite his broken ribs, he was quite convincing in his own defense: how could he have believed that an archpriest was getting into the car, when it was Citizen Chelyustnikov he had brought to the theater? Asked if it was true that on that day—November 21, 1934—he had asked the alleged ecclesiastical personage, i.e., Comrade Chelyustnikov, "And what about Citizen Chelyustnikov, should we wait for him?", Alyosha answered in the negative. Asked if it was true that he had said to the alleged ecclesiastical personage, i.e., Comrade Chelyustnikov, "It will soon be easier to meet a reindeer than a priest in Kiev," he again answered in the negative. Asked if it was true that the alleged ecclesiastical personage, i.e., Comrade Chelyustnikov, had inquired in a grave tone of voice, "And why do you need priests, my son?", he, A. T. Kashalov, answered, "To pray for sinful souls," the answer was again in the negative.

At 5:30 the black limousine stopped in front of the

unlit entrance of the church. The archpriest Chelyustnikov raised the skirts of his robe; for a moment there was a flash of his shiny raspberry-colored boots. "Do you get it now, you fool?" Chelyustnikov asked Alyosha, who was gaping in bewilderment first at his beard and then at his boots. "Now do you get it?"

THE CENSER

"The service began a few minutes before seven," writes Chelyustnikov, who actually gives us a detailed account of the ceremony. (But a certain creative need to add to the living document some possibly unnecessary color, sound, and smell—this decadent Holy Trinity of the moderns—urges me to imagine what is not in Chelyustnikov's text: the flickering and crackling of the candles in silver candelabras brought from the treasury of the Kiev museum—and here again, the document becomes intertwined with our imagined picture; the reflection of the flames on the saints' ghostly faces in the arched apse, on the folds of the long robe of the Virgin Mother in the mosaic, and on the purple cloak with three blazing white crosses; the shimmer of black and gold on the halos and frames of the icons, on the church vessels, the chalice, and the crown, and on the censer swung in half-darkness to the accompaniment of its squeaking chains, while the smell of incense, the soul of the evergreen, merged with the sour smell of hops and malt.) "The minute Comrade Rilsky ran into the church," continues Chelyustnikov, "and began to cross himself, I picked up the censer and began to swing it over the heads of our congregation. I pretended not to notice the arrival of the new believers, although in the half-darkness, through the incense smoke, I could clearly make out the bald spot of Comrade M. and the bristly hair of

Citizen Herriot. Quietly, on tiptoe, they walked to the middle
of the church, and stopped there. The stage fright I had felt
when they suddenly entered had left me and, still swinging
the censer, I moved toward them, mumbling. Citizen Herriot's hands were folded, not as in prayer, but one fist in the
other near the groin, tightly squeezing his Basque beret. After
I swung the censer over them, I continued another few steps
and turned around: Citizen Herriot looked at the ceiling,
then leaned over toward his interpreter, who was leaning
toward Comrade Pyasnikov. Then I swung the censer over
Nastasia Fedotevna, who knelt down and lowered her head,
which was covered with a black kerchief. Without moving,
she threw me a quick glance full of encouragement, which
erased the last traces of my anxiety. (Not a shadow left on
her face from this morning's fear.) Zhelma Chavchavadze,
her hands folded in prayer and her head also wrapped in a
black kerchief, was kneeling beside Nastasia Fedotevna. She
was the wife of Comrade Pyasnikov, and herself an old Party
member. Her eighteen-year-old daughter, Heva, a member
of the Komsomol, was kneeling beside her mother. Except
for an old woman whose face I didn't know and whose presence I couldn't explain, all the faces were familiar: next to
Comrade Alya, who brought us tea that morning in Comrade
Pyasnikov's office, sat the editorial staff and the secretaries
of the Provincial Committee, while some of the women, those
I couldn't place, were without a doubt the wives of comrades
from the Cheka.* I have to admit that without exception all
played their roles with discipline and dedication. Along with
the above-mentioned, here are the names of the rest of the
comrades, since, as I said, I believe that their contribution is
no less important than my own." (There follow forty names,

* Chelyustnikov always uses this word (denoting the Soviet secret police of
1917–22).

interspersed here and there with the comment "with wife.")
"With twelve workers from the cultural brigade and their
two bodyguards, this makes a total of sixty *believers*." After
listing the names, Chelyustnikov concludes: "Comrade Herriot and his retinue stayed in the church for only five minutes,
although it seemed to me they stayed a full fifteen."

THE EXPLANATION OF THE CIRCUS

The frozen ritual of the liturgy was still in progress as in a
fresco—where in the ecstasy of prayer believers first lower
their gaze toward earth, the mother of hell, and then raise it
to heaven, the seat of Paradise—when Herriot and his en-
tourage tiptoed out to look at the famous frescoes painted
along the circular staircases. An art historian, Lydia Krupenick, engaged for this occasion, explained to Herriot in impeccable French (on which he sincerely congratulated her) the
presence of profane scenes in the temple of God—an enigma
that could not escape the attention of the curious visitor.
"Although the circular staircases are some distance from the
shrine, a fact Comrade Herriot can verify for himself, they
are nevertheless an integral part of the church and in this
light, as we see it, the presence of circus scenes in the temple
of God should have astonished and scandalized the priests.
Mais ce sont là des scrupules tout modernes," continued Lydia
Krupenick, "*aussi étrangers aux Byzantins du onzième siécle
qu'aux imagiers et aux huchiers de vos cathédrales gothiques.*
Just as the piety of your ancestors was not in the least of-
fended by the obscene and often grotesque carvings of gar-
goyles and on misericords, so the introduction of secular
painting into churches did not seem in the least scandalous
in the eyes of our pious ancestors. It is known," continued
Lydia Krupenick, as Comrade Herriot nodded his head, star-

ing at the frescoes, particularly drawn to the musical instruments, "it is known that in Constantinople, during the reign
of the iconoclasts, the faces of Christ and the saints were replaced with various satanic scenes: horse races and bloody
spectacles of hunts for wild beasts and human beings." (Comrade Herriot nodded his head, turning his beret in his hands
like a schoolboy.) "While making this comparison, we
shouldn't forget," Lydia Krupenick continued in her charm-
ing voice, which nevertheless seemed to conceal a certain
anger, "other cultural monuments in the West with similar
motifs—for example, the ceiling of the palatine chapel in
Palermo, which depicts the same profane motifs as Saint
Sophia of Kiev: the fighting of athletes, and slaves playing
flutes and reed pipes. And finally, we shouldn't lose sight of
the fact that Saint Sophia of Kiev was, *aussi bien comme les
chapelles de vos rois normands,* a palatine church, and that
the circular staircases led to the apartments of the princes.
Seen in this light, the profane themes were perfectly appro-
priate, *n'est-ce pas?*"

Comrade Herriot, whose feet were cold,* looked at the
frescoes silently, sunk in contemplation.

THE MECHANICAL LIONS

The next day, still fresh from the impact of the trip, sitting
in a warm compartment of the Kiev-Riga-Königsberg sleeping car, feverish and wrapped in blankets, Édouard Herriot
recorded his first impressions in his notebook. Only one fact
(one that relates to our story) marred the purity of his ob-

---

* It is a known fact that Herriot returned ill from this trip, and that he barely
survived. One malicious contributor to *Charivari* wrote in this connection
that Herriot doubtless became ill "while visiting cold churches and overheated
palaces." This allusion provoked much vehement commentary at the time.

servations: the presence of beggars in front of Saint Sophia. He formulated his perplexity in the following way: "These beggars in front of the church, most of them lame and old, but some very young and seemingly healthy, who flocked around us as we left the splendid Saint Sophia, are no doubt that tenacious race of Russian paupers and idiots who gave old Russia its bizarre fauna." (There follow comments on the tasks awaiting the young nation.)

That same detail about beggars (and this is the only reason we mention it) we find also in Chelyustnikov: "As we left the church, we arrested a bunch of parasites who had swooped down on us from out of nowhere, probably attracted by the smell of incense."

Leafing through his notes (from which emanated faces, landscapes, conversations, an entire world so similar to, and yet so different from, the one that existed twelve years earlier, when he had first visited Russia), Herriot tried to condense his impressions, to reduce them to essentials. With his typical pragmatism and wit, he decided that the simplest and most efficient way to do so (for now) would be to repeat the dedication that appeared in his book twelve years ago, as a symbol of the consistency of his views, and thereby silence the malicious. He would repeat it *in extenso,* the same way he wrote it then, in November 1922, and address it to the same person: Élie-Joseph Bois, editor-in-chief of *Petit Parisien.* To confirm the validity of this decision, he took out of his briefcase a leather-bound copy of his book, the last of the twenty copies of the special edition (*il a été tiré de cet ouvrage 20 exemplaires sur Alfa réservé à Monsieur Herriot*), and glanced at the dedication (which we will give here in translation, thereby losing much of the authenticity and style of the original): "Dear friend: When I set off for Russia not only was I heaped with insults from our most prominent critics, but they fore-

saw the worst misfortune befalling me. They saw in me the
very image of that wretched monk who during the Middle
Ages set out from Lyons to convert the Tartars and Khans.
That was the time when the princes of Moscow, to frighten
their visitors, would hide mechanical lions under their
thrones, whose duty it was to growl at the right moment and
in the right place during the conversation. But you, my dear
friend, were prepared to understand my intentions and to
believe in my impartiality. I am returning from a journey
that passed with ridiculous ease. They didn't signal their
mechanical lions to growl at me. I was able to observe everything freely and in peace. I edited my notes unconcerned as
to whether I would please someone or not. And I dedicate
them to you as a sign of recognition: accept them. Sincerely
yours, Édouard Herriot." Satisfied with his decision, Herriot
set the book aside and continued to stare at what he called
"the melancholy of the Russian landscape."

(The consequences of Herriot's second journey to Russia are of historical significance and therefore outside the
interest of our story.)

POST FESTUM

A. L. Chelyustnikov was arrested in Moscow in September
1938, four years after the murder of Kirov (and in connection with it), and a little less than four years after the Herriot
incident. He was sitting in a movie theater when the usherette
approached him and whispered that he was urgently wanted
outside. Chelyustnikov got up, adjusted his holster, and
walked out into the lobby. "Comrade Chelyustnikov," a
stranger said to him, "you are urgently needed at the Provincial Committee. A car is waiting." Chelyustnikov swore
inwardly, thinking that it involved another big comedy like

the one concocted four years ago, and for which he had received a medal and a promotion. He got into the car without suspecting anything. He was then disarmed, handcuffed, and taken to Lubyanka prison. He was beaten and tortured for three months, but he would not sign a declaration that he had sabotaged the Soviet rule, that he had participated in the conspiracy against Kirov, or that he had joined the Trotskyites in Spain. They left him in solitary for another ten days to think it over: sign the confession or his wife would be arrested and their one-year-old daughter taken to an orphanage. Chelyustnikov finally broke down and signed the declaration, admitting the charges made in the indictment—among them, that he was a member of a conspiracy led by Avram Romanich Shram. He got ten years. In the prison camp he met an old NKVD acquaintance alongside whom he had fought earlier in Spain. Chelyustnikov became an informer. He was rehabilitated in 1958. Status: Married, three children. In 1963, with a group of tourists, he traveled to Bordeaux, Lyons, and Paris. In Lyons he visited the memorial library dedicated to its famous mayor, and wrote in the guest book: "An admirer of the work of Édouard Herriot." Signature: A. L. Chelyustnikov.

THE MAGIC CARD DEALING

FOR KARL STEINER

Dr. Taube, Karl Georgievich Taube, was murdered on December 5, 1956, less than two weeks after his formal rehabilitation, and three weeks after his return from Norilsk prison camp. (Not counting his imprisonment during interrogation, Taube had spent seventeen years in prison camps.) This murder was not solved until June 1960, when they arrested in Moscow one Kostik Korshunidze, called "the Artist" or "the Eagle," the top safe-cracker in the country, respected by the underworld as the king of thieves. Captain Morozov, who conducted Kostik's interrogation, was surprised by his behavior: Kostik was trembling. The same Kostik who in his earlier interrogations had talked about himself and his work with the pride and dignity of a master craftsman. In hopeless situations he would even confess, not without pride, to things they didn't question him about: a robbery (for example, the burglary of the Kazan post office) that he had committed two or three years earlier. It was all the easier to get a confession out of Kostik because this brave nighthawk and master thief had one weakness, which, although very human, was seemingly at odds with the rest of his life: Kostik couldn't take beatings. Even a mere threat—the raised voice or the raised hand of the interrogator—reduced Kostik the Artist, the Eagle, to a rag of a man. And you can't wring a confession out of a rag. Captain Morozov, who had already met Kostik twice (once in the prison camp as an informer, and once soon after as a burglar), knew, therefore, how one *should not* talk to him (except in dire need, of course). If they promised not to beat him or shout at him (which insulted his dignity and destroyed his brain cells), Kostik would relate, inside out and in minute technical detail, all his undertakings. He was a born actor—indeed, an inspired one. At one time during his tempestuous life he had belonged to an amateur theatrical company, where he had added some refinement to his crude vocabulary. Later he broadened his acting experience in prison camps as a member of the culture brigade, a director, an actor, and an informer. Incidentally, Kostik thought of his prison term as an inseparable part of his work, just as former revolutionaries regarded theirs as "universities"; his philosophy was not, therefore, at odds with his life style. "Between two great *roles*" (his word) "there is a logical gap which you have to fill as well as you can." It must be granted that during the time of Kostik Korshunidze's greatest triumph, from the 1930's to the 1950's, prison was for him, as for so many other thieves of all kinds, only an extension of "freedom." Millions of politicals were exposed to all the whims and idiosyncrasies of this group, the so-called socially acceptable. The boldest and most fantastic dreams of a thief were fulfilled in the labor camps: the former masters, around whose dachas great and petty burglars had circled, now became servants, "adjutants," and slaves of the former exiles from paradise; and empresses of justice, women ministers and judges, became mistresses and slaves of those whom formerly they had judged, and to whom they had preached about social justice and class consciousness, quoting Gorky, Makarenko, and other classics. It was, in short, a golden age for criminals, especially those whose name in this new hierarchy was surrounded by the aura of the master craftsman, as was the case with Kostik Korshunidze, called the Artist. The king of the underworld is a real king only in the underworld; but not only did Kostik's former masters work for him, but whole legions of hardened criminals submitted to his will. It was sufficient for Kostik to give a hint of his needs, whether by a word or a glance, and the raspberry-colored boots of the former Chekist Chelyustnikov would flash on the feet of a new owner (Kostik), or, through the kindness and mercy of the cook, a former pimp and murderer, the fair-skinned Nastasia Fedotevna, the wife of the (former) secretary of the Provincial Committee, would be fattened and brought to Kostik, since the Artist liked plump ladies: "Fair and ripe, this is the best type of our Russian women."

But since Kostik continued to tremble even after his long confession (although the interrogator did not raise his voice, and moreover, to put him at ease and at the same time to deride him, addressed him as "Citizen"), Captain Morozov, prompted more by a strange inspiration than by a tip from one of his informers, ordered the experts to compare Kostik's fingerprints with those found on a jimmy used as the murder weapon on one Karl Georgievich Taube four years before in Tumen. The result was positive. Thus the veil over an apparently senseless murder was at least partially lifted.

PICTURES FROM THE ALBUM

Karl Georgievich Taube was born in 1899 in Esztergom, Hungary. Despite the meager data covering his earliest years, the provincial bleakness of the Middle European towns at the turn of the century emerges clearly from the depths of time: the gray, one-story houses with back yards that the sun in its slow journey divides with a clear line of demarcation into quarters of murderous light and damp, moldy shade resembling darkness; the rows of black locust trees which at the beginning of spring exude, like thick cough syrups and cough drops, the musky smell of childhood diseases; the cold, baroque gleam of the pharmacy where the Gothic of the white porcelain vessels glitters; the gloomy high school with the paved yard (green, peeling benches, broken swings resembling gallows, and whitewashed wooden outhouses); the municipal building painted Maria-Theresa yellow, the color of the dead leaves and autumn roses from ballads played at dusk by the gypsy band in the open-air restaurant of the Grand Hotel.

Like so many provincial children, the pharmacist's son, Karl Taube, dreamed about that happy day when, through the thick lenses of his glasses, he would see his town from the bird's-eye view of departure and for the last time, as one looks through a magnifying glass at dried-out and absurd yellow butterflies from one's school collection: with sadness and disgust.

In the autumn of 1920, at Budapest's Eastern Station he boarded the first-class car of the Budapest-Vienna Express. The moment the train pulled out, the young Karl Taube waved once more to his father (who was disappearing like a dark blot in the distance, waving his silk handkerchief), then quickly carried his leather suitcase into the third-class car and sat down among the workers.

CREDO

Two important factors prevent a better understanding of this tumultuous period in the life of Karl Taube: his illegal activities and the numerous aliases he used. We know that he frequented émigré cafés, that he collaborated with Novsky, that he socialized not only with Hungarian, but with German and Russian émigrés as well, and that under the aliases of Károly Beatus and Kiril Beitz he wrote articles for left-wing papers. An incomplete and thoroughly unreliable list of his works from that period includes some hundred and thirty treatises and articles, and we cite here only several that can be clearly identified because of a certain vehemence of style (which is only another name for class hatred): *Religious Capital; The Red Sun, or Of Certain Principles; The Inheritance of Béla Kun; White and Bloody Terror; Credo.*

His biographer and acquaintance of those émigré days, Dr. Tamás Ungváry, gives us the following description of Taube: "In 1921, when I met Comrade Beitz in the Viennese editorial office of the magazine *Ma,* which was edited at that time by the indecisive Lajos Kassák, I was most surprised by Beitz's modesty and calm. Although I knew he was the author of the *Bloody Terror, Credo,* and other texts, I was unable to reconcile the intensity and force of his style with that calm, quiet man wearing thick glasses who seemed somehow shy and ill at ease. And strangely," continued Ungváry, "I heard him more often discussing medical problems than political ones. Once, in the laboratory of the clinic where he worked, he showed me neatly lined-up jars containing fetuses in different stages of development; every jar was labeled with the name of a dead revolutionary. On this occasion he told me that he had shown his fetuses to Novsky, who literally became nauseated. This quiet young man, who at twenty-two gave every impression of being a mature man, soon came into conflict not only with the police, who discreetly followed his movements from the start, but with his fellow militants: he thought that our actions weren't efficient enough, and our articles lukewarm." After four years in Vienna, disillusioned by the slow progress of revolutionary ferment, he left for Berlin, which he believed to be "the nucleus and heart of the best émigrés from European prisons." From then until 1934 we lost all trace of him. In some articles written under a pseudonym, it seemed to me, and I don't think I was mistaken, I recognized a sentence of Taube's that sounded "as if it contained a detonator" (as Lukács once said). I know that until his arrest he collaborated with Ernst Thälmann. Then, in the spring of 1935, we read the speech he delivered before the International Forum in Geneva, where he forecast all of the horrors of Dachau and once more warned the world of the danger: "A phantom stalks through Europe, the phantom of fascism." The weaklings who were impressed with the strength of the new Deutschland, her tanned young men and strong Amazons parading to the sounds of stern German marches, were for a moment taken aback, listening to Taube's prophetic words. But only for a moment: then Taube, provoked by a famous French journalist, took off his jacket and, embarrassed but resolute, rolled up his shirt to expose the still-fresh marks of heavy lashes on his back. But once official Nazi propaganda responded by calling Taube's public testimony "Communist provocation," they abandoned their doubts: the spirit of Europe needed new, strong men, and they would arise from blood and flames. So that same journalist, who had been momentarily shocked by the raw wounds, dismissed all doubt and contrary evidence, disgusted by his own weakness and the squeamishness of his Latin race, "which snivels at the mere mention of blood."

THE LONG WALKS

One rainy autumn day in 1935, crossing the Latvian-Soviet border, Dr. Karl Taube again became Kiril Beitz, perhaps wishing to erase once and for all the scars of his moral and physical suffering. He arrived in Moscow (according to Ungváry) on September 15, although another source gives a somewhat later date: October 5. For two months Taube, alias Beitz, walked the streets of Moscow as if under a spell, the frozen rain and snow fogging the thick lenses of his glasses. Evenings he was seen arm in arm with his wife, wandering around the Kremlin wall captivated by the wonder of the electric lights, which illuminated the Moscow night with revolutionary slogans in big red letters. "He wanted to see everything, to see and touch, not only because of his myopia, but to make sure that it wasn't a dream," says K. S. He spent little time in the Lux Hotel—the residence of all the elite European Comintern members, where he was allotted an apartment—and he socialized without much enthusiasm with his former colleagues from Vienna and Berlin. During the two months of these constant wanderings, he got to know Moscow better than any other city in his life; he knew all the housing developments, every street, park, municipal building, and monument, all the bus and streetcar lines. He already knew all the shop signs and slogans: "He learned his Russian," wrote one of his biographers, "through the language of posters and slogans, that same action-speech that he himself most often used."

One day he realized to his dismay that, with the exception of the buttoned-up and formal employees of the Comintern, he actually hadn't met a single Russian. This sudden discovery deeply affected him. He returned from his walk shivering and burning with fever.

According to the testimony of K. S., who spent some six months with Taube in the Norilsk prison camp, this is what happened that day: on the bus on Tver Boulevard, a man sat down beside Taube with whom he wanted to start a conversation; when the man realized Taube was a foreigner, he abruptly got up and changed his seat, mumbling some excuse. The manner in which he did this hit Taube like an electric current, like a sudden revelation. He got off at the next stop and wandered through the city until dawn.

For a week he didn't leave his room on the third floor of the Lux, where his wife nursed him with tea and cough syrup. He emerged from this illness worn and looking much older, and he resolutely knocked on the door of Comrade Chernomordikov, who was in charge of personal matters. "Comrade Chernomordikov," he said in a hoarse, trembling voice, "I don't consider my stay in Moscow a vacation. I want to work." "Be patient a little while longer," said Chernomordikov enigmatically.

BETWEEN ACTS

The least-known period in the life of Dr. Taube, strange as it may seem, is the interval between his arrival in Moscow and his arrest a year later. Some records show that for a period of time he worked for the International Trade Union, after which, at the intervention of Béla Kun (himself in disfavor), he worked as a journalist, then as a translator, and finally as a proofreader attached to the Hungarian section of the Comintern. It is also known that in August 1936 he resided in the Caucasus, where he had accompanied his wife, who had become ill. Ungváry states that it was tuberculosis, while K. S. claims that she was being treated "for nerves." If we accept the latter explanation (and much circumstantial evidence supports it), it points to the hidden and to us unknown spiritual suffering the Taubes experienced during this period. It is difficult to say whether it was a question of disillusionment or a foreboding of the imminent catastrophe. "I am convinced," says K. S., "that for Beitz anything that was happening to him could not have had larger repercussions: he thought, as we all did, that it was a question of a slight misunderstanding relating to him personally, a misunderstanding that had nothing to do with the major and essential currents of history and that, as such, was entirely negligible."

However, one seemingly trivial incident relating to Taube draws our attention: in late September a breathless young man with a cap pulled down over his eyes collided with Taube (who was returning from the print shop) so awkwardly that he knocked his glasses to the pavement; flustered, the young man apologized, and in his haste and confusion stepped on the glasses, smashed them to pieces, and then promptly disappeared.

Dr. Karl Taube, alias Kiril Beitz, was arrested fourteen days after this incident, on November 12, 1936, at 2:35 A.M.

THE BLUNT AX

If the roads of destiny were not so unpredictable in their complex architecture, where the end is never known but only sensed, one might say that, despite his horrible end, Karl Taube was born under a lucky star (provided our thesis is

acceptable that, despite everything, the temporary suffering
of existence is worth more than the final void of nothingness). For those who wanted to kill the revolutionary in
Taube—both in Dachau and in distant Kolyma—did not
want to, or could not, kill the physician in him, the miracle
worker. Here we don't want to develop the heretical and
dangerous thought that could be drawn from this example:
that disease and its shadow, death, are, particularly in the eyes
of tyrants, only the masks of the supernatural, and that doctors are magicians of a kind—all of which is the logical
consequence of a particular view of life.

We know that toward the end of 1936 Dr. Taube spent
some time in Murmansk prison camp, that he was sentenced
to death, that the sentence was reduced to twenty years at
hard labor, and that during the first months he went on a
hunger strike because they had confiscated his glasses. And
that's all. In the spring of 1941, we find him in a nickel mine
in the far north. At that point he was wearing a white hospital coat and, like one of the righteous, visiting his numerous
patients sentenced to slow death. Two operations had made
him famous in the camp: one performed on his former tor-
turer from Lubyanka, Lieutenant Krichenko (now a prisoner), on whom he successfully operated when his appendix
burst; and the other on a criminal whom they called Segidulin; of the four fingers Segidulin had cut with a blunt ax to
free himself from the horrendous torture of the nickel mine,
Taube saved two. The reaction of the former burglar was
interesting. Having realized that his own surgical undertak-
ing had been unsuccessful, he threatened Taube with a just
punishment: to cut his throat. Only after another criminal,
his bunkmate, had informed him of rumors about the pend-
ing rehabilitation of the socially acceptable (rumors that
turned out to be true) did Segidulin change his mind and

withdraw (at least temporarily) his solemn threat. He must
have realized that in the practice of his profession as a thief
those two fingers would come in handy.

TREATISE ON GAMES OF CHANCE

In the ever-growing testimonials about the hell of the Frozen
Islands, documents describing the mechanism of games of
chance are still rare; and I don't mean the chances of life
and death: the entire literature of the lost continent is actually nothing more than an enlarged metaphor of this Great
Lottery in which winning is rare and losing the rule. It would
be interesting for the modern researcher to study the relation-
ship between these two mechanisms: while the wheel of the
Great Lottery turned relentlessly, like the incarnate principle
of a mythical and evil deity, the victims of this inexorable
merry-go-round, driven by the spirit of an at once platonic
and infernal *imitatio,* emulated the great principle of Chance:
the bands of criminals under the flattering and privileged
label of "socially acceptable" gambled through endless polar
nights for anything they could: money, caps with ear flaps,
boots, a bowl of soup, a piece of bread, a cube of sugar, a
frozen potato, tobacco, a piece of tattooed skin (one's own
or someone else's), a rape, a dagger, a life.

But the history of the prisoners' card games and games
of chance in the new Atlantis remains unwritten. So it may
be useful if I explain briefly (and according to Tarashchenko)
some of the principles of these monstrous games—principles
that in a way are interwoven with this story.

Tarashchenko cites the numerous ways of gambling
among the criminals he observed during the ten years he
spent in various regions of the sunken world (mostly in
Kolyma), of which the least bizarre is perhaps the one played

with lice—a game very similar to the one played in warmer regions with flies: a cube of sugar is placed in front of each player, then everyone waits in grave silence for a fly to land on one of the cubes and so determine the winner and loser, as previously agreed. The lice have the same role, except that the bait here is the player himself, without any artificial props except the stench of his own body and "a lucky break." That is, of course, if it's luck that's involved. For very often the person to whom the louse crawled had the unpleasant duty of cutting the throat of whomever the winner marked as the victim. Equally interesting is the list of prisoners' games and their iconography. Although during the 1940's it was no longer a rarity to see a real deck of cards (stolen or bought from outsiders) in the hands of criminals, nevertheless, says Tarashchenko, the most popular way of gambling was with a handmade (and of course marked) deck, made out of pieces of glued-together newspaper. All kinds of games of chance were played, from the simplest, like skat, poker, and black-jack, to a kind of secret Tarot.

THE DEVIL

The Devil or the Mother represents a whole symbolic coded language very similar to the Marseilles Tarot. It is interest-ing, however, that the hardened criminals, those with longer prison experience, used the handmade cards for another kind of communication: often, instead of using words, they would pick up a card and suddenly, as if by an order, a knife would flash, blood would spill. We have further learned, from the explanation given by a murderer whose confidence had been gained, that the medieval iconography of those cards was mixed with some elements of Eastern and ancient Russian symbolism. In the commonest variation, the number of cards was reduced to twenty-six.

"I never had the opportunity," says Tarashchenko, "to see a clean deck of seventy-eight cards, although arithmetic clearly shows (by the division of seventy-eight by three and two) that it was only a simplified version of the classical Tarot combination. I am convinced that this simplification was the result of purely technical considerations: these cards were easier to make and hide." As for colors (sometimes designated only by the initial letters), they were reduced to four: pink, blue, red, and yellow. Ideographical symbols were made most often in their elementary outlines, which were the following: a Stick (an order, command, head; but also meaning a split skull); a Goblet (mother, vodka, debauchery, alliance); a Dagger (freedom, homosexuality, cut throat); a Gold Coin (murder, torture, solitary). The other symbols and variations were: the Whore, the Queen, the King, the Father, 69, Troika, the Power, the Hanged Man, the Nameless One (Death), the Bowels, the Devil, the Fool, the Star, the Moon, the Sun, the Trial, the Spear (or Anchor). The Devil or the Mother remains essentially only a variation of that anthropocentric game that reached us from the distant mythical regions of the Middle Ages crossed with Asia: spread out, the cards of the Devil represent the Wheel of Fortune, and for a fanatic have the significance of the finger of fate. Tarashchenko concludes: "In the European Tarot, the connection between the symbols of Chiromancy and the Zodiac has not been lost: the tattoos on the chest, back, and bottom of the prisoners have the same meaning that the signs of the Zodiac have for Westerners, and could be connected with the Devil by the same principle." Tertz also raises this connection between tattooing and mythical symbols to a metaphysical plane: "A tattoo: in front, an eagle tearing the breast of Prometheus in his beak; on the back, a dog in an unusual coital position with a lady. Two sides of the same coin. The head and the tail. Light and dark. Tragedy and comedy. A parody of one's own grandeur. The proximity of sex and laughter. Sex and death."

MAKARENKO'S BASTARDS

In the bluish haze of the cell's semidarkness, where clouds of smoke rose in spirals, the four cardplayer-criminals reclined like boyars on bunks infested with bedbugs, turning a dirty straw between their chipped yellow teeth or sucking tobacco wrapped into a thick, slobbery cigar. A colorful mob of spectators watched with admiration the faces of the notorious murderers and their tattooed chests and arms—because they couldn't look at the cards, which were only for the masters; they wouldn't dare look at a card except when it was played, or it might cost dearly. But it was a great privilege to be at this criminal Olympus, in the presence of those who in a religious silence held in their hands the fate of others—a fate that, through this magic card dealing, assumed in the eyes of the spectators the guise of chance. It was a great privilege to stoke their stove, to hand them water, to steal a towel for them, to pick lice from their shirts, or, at a single wink, to leap at one of those wretches in the crowd and silence him once and for all, making sure he wouldn't, in his incessant ravings against heaven, interrupt the relentless flow of the game—a game in which the nameless arcanum with the number thirteen, marked with the color of blood and fire, could cut short any illusion or reduce it to ashes. So it is lucky to be up there on the bunks, in the presence of the tattooed gods, the Eagle, the Snake, the

Dragon, and the Monkey, and their awful curses, which couple one's mother (the only thing a criminal holds sacred) with a dog or with the devil. Thus out of the blue haze emerged the picture of those criminals, Makarenko's bastards, who, under the mythical name "socially acceptable," have staged shows for the past fifty years in the theaters of the capitals of Europe, with their proletarian caps cocked rakishly to one side and holding red carnations between their teeth— riffraff who in the ballet *The Lady and the Hooligan* would perform their famous pirouette of the transformation of a hooligan into a troubadour or into a sheep docilely drinking water from the palm of someone's hand.

THE MONKEY AND THE EAGLE

Holding the cards between the stumps of his left hand (by which, now and forever, it would be easy to recognize the famous criminal, while in his police file the fingerprints of the pointer and middle fingers would be mysteriously missing), Segidulin, naked to the waist and sporting on his hairless chest a tattoo of a masturbating monkey, watched Kostik with bloodshot eyes and plotted revenge. There was for a moment deadly silence up there among the criminals, as well as below, among those convicted of the far more dangerous crime: thinking. The spectators held their breath, didn't move or bat an eyelid, but stared somewhere out into space, petrified, with a cigarette butt sizzling on their lips (but no one would dare spit it out, move his head, or scratch his hairy chest crawling with lice). The exhausted and half- dead prisoners below stopped whispering: something was happening. A criminal is dangerous when silent. The Wheel of Fortune had stopped. Someone's mother would grieve.

And that was all they knew, all they could possibly know;
except for this horrendous language of silence and curses,
the politicals were altogether unfamiliar with the coded
speech of criminals, and the words whose meaning they did
know were of no help anyway because in thieves' slang the
meanings are shifted: God means the devil and the devil
means God. Segidulin waited for the chief to show his cards;
it was his turn. Kruminsh and Gadyashvili, whose names
were recorded in the history of the underworld, put aside
their cards and were now watching the duel between the
Monkey and the Eagle with pleasurable trepidation. (Segidulin was the former chief whose place was usurped while
he was in the hospital by Kostik, known as the Artist and,
to friends, as the Eagle.)

Below, everyone felt uneasy: the silence on the thieves'
bunks had gone on for too long; everyone was waiting for
the shriek and the curse. However, the duel was between the
two chiefs, the old and the new, and so the rules of the
game were somewhat different. First, there was the language
of competition and provocation. "Well, Monkey," said the
Eagle, "now you can stick your left hand into pockets." A
second or two passed before Segidulin, the former chief and
famous murderer, could respond to the terrible insult. "We'll
see about that later, Eagle. Now show your cards." Someone
coughed, no doubt one of the former co-players; who else
could have been so careless? "Which hand should I use,
Monkey, left or right?" asked Kostik. "Listen, Bird, you
better show your cards, even if you have to hold them in
your beak." The bunks creaked, then all was silent. Suddenly
Kostik cursed his opponent's crippled mother, the only thing
a criminal holds sacred. Everyone understood, even those
who were unfamiliar with thieves' slang: the master had
lost; someone's mother would grieve.

THE BITCH

The chances are that it will never be known who told Dr. Taube how the famous card game in which he was given a death sentence ended, and in which the sly Monkey, aided by luck, defeated the royal Eagle, the master of masters, Kostik Korshunidze. The most likely hypothesis is that one of the thief-informers—in a nightmarish dilemma whether to expose himself to the disfavor of the authorities or to one of his own kind—finally opted, gambling with fate, for the illusory and treacherous protection of his temporary masters, and reported the matter to the authorities of the prison camp. Taube, who to some degree enjoyed the goodwill of the prison camp's supervisor, a certain Panov, famous for his cruelty, departed with the first transport of prisoners for Kolyma, some three thousand kilometers to the northeast. The hypothesis offered by Tarashchenko seems entirely plausible to me: Segidulin himself informed Taube through one of his underlings. The explanation of Segidulin's action also seems logical to me: the Monkey wanted to humiliate the Eagle. If the one whom fortune did not favor that day, who took upon himself the solemn duty of liquidating Taube on Segidulin's account, were unable to carry out his sacred duty, he would bear the shameful label "bitch" for a long time. And to be a "bitch" means to be despised by all, which is intolerable to a former chief.

Kostik, called the Artist or the Eagle, dragged around and howled like a leprous bitch the very next day, when, returning from the mine (where he had become the foreman and the scourge of the prisoners), he learned that Taube had been transported. "The one you *took upon your-self* has married another," Segidulin, the new chief, said to

him in his hissing voice. "You're lying, Monkey," answered
Kostik, pale as a ghost, but one could see by the expression
on his face that he believed Segidulin's words.

THE JIMMY

Kostik, the molted Eagle, the once notorious safe-cracker
and ex-chief, dragged around like this for eight years, bowed
down like a leprous bitch, hiding the eagle pecking at his
liver, changing prison camps and prison camp hospitals,
where various keys, little bundles of wire, spoons, and rusted
nails were extracted from his stomach. For eight years Segidulin's shadow hovered over him like an evil omen, sending
him messages which awaited him at various transit stations,
and which called him by his real name: "Bitch." And then
one day, now a free man (if one could call a man who lived
under the terrible burden of humiliation "free"), he received
a letter from someone who knew his secret. The letter was
mailed from Moscow and took ten days to reach Maklakov.
In the envelope, postmarked November 23, 1956, there was
a jumbled news item (without the date), from which, however, Kostik could figure out the information he needed:
Dr. Taube, an old Party member and former member of the
Comintern known as Kiril Beitz, had been rehabilitated, and
upon leaving the prison camp he had become director of a
hospital in Tumen. (Tarashchenko's hypothesis that the news
item was sent by Segidulin seems to me again entirely plausible; the safe-cracker must become a murderer or he would
remain a "bitch"—satisfaction enough for one who had enjoyed his revenge for years.) Kostik left the very same day.
How he managed to get from Arkhangelsk to Tumen
without the necessary documents, within three days, is of no
consequence here. From the Tumen railroad station he pro-

ceeded to the hospital on foot. During the subsequent investigation, the porter remembered that on the night of the murder a strange man had asked for Dr. Taube. The porter couldn't remember his face, because the stranger's cap obscured his eyes. Taube, who had arrived in Tumen several days before, after working for two years as a free man in the Norilsk prison camp, slept on the hospital premises, and was on duty that night. When Kostik entered the room, Taube was standing at the table and opening a can of tuna fish. The radio was on softly, and Taube didn't hear the padded door open. Kostik took a jimmy out of his sleeve and delivered three powerful blows to his skull, not even looking at his face. Then, without haste, and probably with relief, he passed by the porter, a former Cossack who was so full of vodka that he rocked slightly while sleeping in an upright position, as though in a saddle.

THE LAST HONORS

Only two persons escorted Dr. Taube's coffin: his housekeeper, Frau Else, a Volga German (one of the rare surviving specimens of this human flora), and a devout and somewhat unbalanced woman of Tumen who attended every funeral. Frau Else was the doctor's housekeeper from the far-off Moscow days, when Taube first came to Russia. At the time of his death she must have been seventy. Although her native language was German, as was Taube's, they always spoke to each other in Russian. There were two reasons for this: in the first place the desire of the Taube family to make the adjustment to the new environment easier, and also as a form of extreme politeness, which essentially amounted to a more elegant form of fear.

But now there was no one left alive in the doctor's family

(his wife had died in the prison camp, and his son had been killed in action), so Frau Else reverted to her native language: her dry, purple lips were fervently whispering a prayer in German. Meanwhile, the devout woman of Tumen was praying in Russian for the soul of the servant of God, Karl Georgievich, whose name was written in gold letters on the funeral wreath ordered by the hospital collective.

This took place in the Tumen cemetery on the bitterly cold afternoon of December 7, 1956.

Distant and mysterious are the ways that brought together the Georgian murderer and Dr. Taube. As distant and mysterious as the ways of God.

A TOMB FOR BORIS DAVIDOVICH

IN MEMORY OF LEONID ŠEJKA

History recorded him as Novsky, which is only a pseudonym
(or, more precisely, one of his pseudonyms). But what immediately spawns doubt is the question: did history really
record him? In the index of the *Granat Encyclopedia,* among
the 246 authorized biographies and autobiographies of great
men and participants in the Revolution, his name is missing.
In his commentary on this encyclopedia, Haupt notes that all
the important figures of the Revolution are represented, and
laments only the "surprising and inexplicable absence of
Podvoysky." Even he fails to make any allusion to Novsky,
whose role in the Revolution was more significant than that
of Podvoysky. So in a "surprising and inexplicable" way this
man whose political principles gave validity to a rigorous
ethic, this vehement internationalist, appears in the revolutionary chronicles as a character without a face or a voice.

In this text, however fragmentary and incomplete, I
shall try to bring to life the memory of the extraordinary

and enigmatic person that was Novsky. Certain omissions—
particularly those concerning the most important period of
his life: the Revolution and the years immediately following
it—could be explained in much the same way the above
commentator explains other biographies: after 1917, his
life merges with public life and becomes "a part of history."
On the other hand, as Haupt points out, we should not forget
that these biographies were written in the late 1920's: hence
the significant omissions, discretion, and haste. Haste before
death, we might add.

The ancient Greeks had an admirable custom: for anyone who perished by fire, was swallowed by a volcano, buried
by lava, torn to pieces by beasts, devoured by sharks, or
whose corpse was scattered by vultures in the desert, they
built so-called cenotaphs, or empty tombs, in their home-
lands; for the body is only fire, water, or earth, whereas the
soul is the Alpha and the Omega, to which a shrine should
be erected.

Right after Christmas of 1885, the Czar's Second Cavalry Regiment halted on the west bank of the Dnieper to
catch their breath and celebrate the feast of the Epiphany.
Prince Vyazemsky, a cavalry colonel, emerged from the icy
water with the symbol of Christ in the form of a silver cross.
Prior to that, the soldiers had shattered the thick crust of ice
for some twenty meters around with dynamite; the water
was the color of steel. The young Prince Vyazemsky had
refused to let them tie a rope around his waist. He crossed
himself, his blue eyes gazing at the clear winter sky, and
jumped into the water. His emergence from the icy whirlpools was first celebrated with salvos, and then with the
popping of the corks of champagne bottles in the improvised

officers' canteen set up in an elementary school building.
The soldiers received their holiday ration of seven hundred
grams of Russian cognac each: the personal gift of Prince
Vyazemsky to the Second Cavalry. Drinking began right
after the religious service in the village church and continued
until late in the afternoon. David Abramovich was the only
soldier not present at the service. They say that during that
time he was lying in the warm manger of the stables, reading
the Talmud, which, given the profusion of associations, seems
dubious to me. One of the soldiers noticed his absence and
a search began. They found him in the shed (in the stables,
according to some) with the untouched bottle of cognac
beside him. They forced him to drink the liquor given him
by the grace of the Czar, stripped him to the waist so as not
to desecrate the uniform, and set about flogging him with a
knout. Finally, when he was unconscious, they tied him to a
horse and dragged him to the Dnieper. A thin crust had
already formed where they had previously broken the ice.
Having tied him around the waist with horse whips so he
wouldn't drown, they pushed him into the icy water. When
they finally pulled him out, blue and half dead, they poured
the remainder of the cognac down his throat and then,
holding the silver cross over his forehead, sang in chorus
"The Fruit of Thy Womb." In the evening, while he was
burning with fever, they transferred him from the stables
to the house of Solomon Malamud, the village teacher.
Malamud's sixteen-year-old daughter coated the wounds on
the back of the unfortunate private with cod-liver oil. Before
leaving with his regiment, which was being dispatched that
morning to crush an uprising, David Abramovich, still
feverish, swore to her that he would come back. He kept his
promise. From this romantic encounter, whose authenticity

we have no reason to doubt, Boris Davidovich was born, he who would go down in history under the name of Novsky, B. D. Novsky.

In the archives of the Czar's secret police, the Okhrana, three birth dates are entered: 1891, 1893, 1896. This was not just the result of the false documents revolutionaries used (a few coins to the clerk or the priest, and the matter was taken care of); it was one more proof of bureaucratic corruption.

At the age of four he was already able to read and write; at nine his father took him along to the Saratov Tavern near the Jewish market, where at a corner table, by the porcelain spittoon, his father practiced his trade as a lawyer. The place was frequented by retired soldiers of the Czar with flaming red beards and deeply sunken eyes, as well as by converted Jewish merchants in their long greasy caftans, whose Russian names went awkwardly with their Semitic gait (three thousand years of slavery and a long tradition of pogroms had created a gait peculiar to the ghettos). Since he was already more literate than his father, little Boris Davidovich recorded their complaints. In the evening, they say, his mother read the Psalms to him, chanting them. When he was ten, an old estate overseer told him about the peasant uprisings of 1846: a harsh tale in which the knout, saber, and gallows dealt out both justice and injustice. At thirteen, under the influence of Vladimir Soloviev's Antichrist, he ran away from home, but was brought back, escorted by police from a distant station. There follows a sudden and inexplicable gap. We find him at the market selling empty bottles for two kopecks each, then offering smuggled tobacco, matches, and lemons. It is a known fact that at that time his father fell under the dangerous influence of the Nihilists and brought the family to the edge of disaster. (Some insist that tuberculosis played a part in it, probably seeing in the disease the symptoms of a treacherous, organic nihilism.)

At fourteen he worked as an apprentice for a kosher butcher. After a year and a half we find him washing dishes and cleaning samovars in that same tavern where once he recorded legal complaints; at sixteen, classifying artillery shells at the arsenal in Pavlograd; at seventeen, as a dock worker in Riga, reading Leonid Andreyev and Scheller-Mihaylov while out on strike. The same year we find him in the Teodore Kibel box and cardboard factory, where he earned five kopecks a day.

His biography does not lack information; what is puzzling is the chronology (which his aliases and the dizzying succession of places make only more difficult). In February 1913 we find him in Baku as a fireman's helper on a steam engine; in September of the same year, among the leaders of a strike in a wallpaper factory in Ivanovo-Voznesensk; in October, among the organizers of the street demonstrations in St. Petersburg. Nor are details lacking: the police on horses scattering the demonstrators with sabers and black leather whips, the Junker variation of a knout. Boris Davidovich, then known as Bezrabotny, managed to escape through the side entrance of a brothel on Dolgorukovska Street. He spent several months with tramps in the public baths, which were undergoing renovation, then joined a terrorist group preparing for assassinations with bombs. In the early spring of 1914, we find him, as the night guard of the public baths, with chains on his ankles, on the hard road to Vladimir Central Prison. Ill with a high fever, he passed through the successive stages of the trip in a kind of fog. At Narym, where they took the chains off his thin and calloused ankles, he managed to escape in an oarless dinghy he found tied to the bank. He surrendered the dinghy to the fast current of the river, but soon realized that the unbridled force of nature, like that of humanity, does not submit to dreams and curses: they found him five miles downstream, where a whirlpool had capsized him. He had spent several hours in the icy water, perhaps aware he was experiencing a repetition of his family legend: on the bank of the river, a thin crust of ice still remained. In June, under the name Jacob Mauzer, he was again sentenced to six years for organizing a secret terrorist group among the prisoners; during his three months in Tomsky Prison, he listened to the screams and last words of those being led to their death; in the shadow of the gallows he read Antonio Labriola's texts on historical materialism.

In the spring of 1912, in elegant St. Petersburg salons, where talk of Rasputin was growing ever more anxious, a young engineer named Zemlyanikov appeared, dressed in a light-colored suit in the lastest fashion, with a dark orchid pinned to his lapel, a dandy's hat, a walking stick, and a monocle. This dandy, with his fine bearing, broad shoulders, small, trim beard, and thick dark hair, boasted of his connections, talked of Rasputin with derision, and claimed to be a personal acquaintance of Leonid Andreyev. From here on, the story unfolds in a classical manner: suspicious at first of the young braggart, the ladies discovered his indisputable charm and began to pester him with invitations, especially after he had proved at least one of his stories. Marya Gregorovna Popko, the wife of a high official of the Czar, spotted him one day in the suburbs, sitting in a black lacquered carriage, giving orders while bending over his plans. The news that Zemlyanikov was the chief engineer responsible for setting up electric cables and installations in St.

Petersburg (a fact historically verified) only added to his popularity and increased the number of invitations. Zemlyanikov arrived in the black lacquered carriage at the appointed times, drank champagne, and talked about Viennese high society with undisguised sympathy and a certain nostalgia; then, promptly at ten, he would leave the company of the tipsy ladies and get into the carriage. The understandable suspicion that Zemlyanikov had a high-society common-law wife (and a child, according to some)—a suspicion he himself encouraged by his sudden departures promptly at ten— could never be proven. However, many saw this as a part of his eccentricity, especially after that famous blunder in the salon of the Gerasimovs, where, while Olga Mihailovna was singing an aria, Zemlyanikov looked at his silver pocket watch and, to everyone's astonishment, left the concert without waiting for the end of the aria.

Zemlyanikov's sudden and abrupt leave-takings from St. Petersburg's salons did not surprise anyone. It was common knowledge that, as chief engineer, he often traveled abroad: a responsibility he alleviated by using the occasion to renew his wardrobe with elegant accessories and, along with suitable presents, to bring some new anecdote about fashionable life outside Russia. Thus his absence from a famous soirée that fall elicited only regret, the more so since Zemlyanikov had confirmed his attendance by telegram. But this time his absence lasted a little too long, and it could rightfully be said that Zemlyanikov's presence in St. Petersburg salons was only a seasonal fad, one of those that undergo the sad fate of sudden oblivion. (His place was filled by a handsome young cadet who brought fresh anecdotes from the Court, from the immediate presence of Rasputin himself, but who, unlike Zemlyanikov, had no other duties and so would entertain the company till dawn.) The astonishment was

greater when that same Marya Gregorovna Popko, who
seemed to enjoy roaming the city in her carriage like a queen,
spied a familiar face on Stolpinska Street among the frozen
and starved prisoners who were sweeping the pavement. She
approached this man and dropped a coin in his hand; without
doubt, it was Zemlyanikov.

So the ghost of Engineer Zemlyanikov had returned
again to the salons, and briefly threatened to undermine the
fame of Rasputin. It was not too difficult to establish certain
facts: Zemlyanikov had used his frequent trips abroad for
thoroughly disloyal purposes; on his last return from Berlin,
under the silk shirts and expensive suits in his black leather
suitcases, the border police had discovered some fifty Brownings of German make. But what Marya Gregorovna couldn't
have known—and for its revelation, some twenty years had
to elapse (until the discovery of the Okhrana archives stolen
by Ambassador Malakov)—elicited a much greater shock:
Zemlyanikov was the organizer of and a participant in the
famous "expropriation" of the mail car, when several million rubles came into the hands of the revolutionaries; in
addition to the confiscated Brownings, he had on three
separate occasions transported explosives and arms to Russia;
as the editor of *Eastern Dawn,* which was printed on cigarette
paper in a secret printing shop, he personally transported
rubber stencils in his black suitcase; the spectacular assassinations of the last five or six years were his doing (they
were different from all other assassinations: the bombs
assembled in Zemlyanikov's secret workshop reduced their
victims to a heap of bloody flesh); as a consequence of
his arrogant behavior (doubtless simulated), the workers
assigned to him hated him; by his own admission he
dreamed of creating a bomb the size of a walnut but with

tremendous destructive force (an ideal, they say, to which he came dangerously close); the police believed him dead after the assassination of Governor von Launitz (three witnesses confirmed that the head displayed in an alcohol-filled jar was Zemlyanikov's; the appearance of the demonic Azef was needed to ascertain that the head in the alcohol, already somewhat shrunken, was not identical to the "Assyrian skull" of Zemlyanikov); he had escaped twice from prison and once from a labor camp (the first time by smashing through the wall of the prison cell; the second time by escaping during bathing time, dressed as the prison supervisor whom he left naked); after his last arrest, he crossed the border in a Jewish one-horse cart, disguised as a traveling merchant, by way of the famous Vilkomirsky smugglers' road; he lived with a false passport under the name M. V. Zemlyanikov, but his real name was Boris Davidovich Malamud, alias B. D. Novsky.

After an obvious gap in our sources (with which we don't want to burden the reader, so he can retain a pleasant but false satisfaction in believing that this is a story like any other, which, fortunately for the author, is usually equated with the power of his imagination), we find him in an insane asylum in Malinovsk, among severely disturbed and dangerous lunatics, from which, disguised as a high school student, he escaped on a bicycle to Batum. Undoubtedly he faked his madness, its certification by two eminent doctors notwithstanding; even the police were aware of this, retaining the two doctors as sympathizers of the Revolution. His later whereabouts are more or less known: one early September morning in 1913, just before dawn, Novsky boarded a ship and, hidden among tons of eggs, headed for Paris via Constantinople. There, during the day we find him in the Russian Library on the Avenue des Gobelins and in the Musée Guimet, where he studied the philosophy of history and religion; and in the evening, in La Rotonde in Montparnasse with a glass of beer, wearing "the most elegant hat to be found in all Paris." (Bruce Lockhart's allusion to Novsky's hat is not, however, without its political implications: it is common knowledge that Novsky was a functionary of the powerful union of Jewish hatmakers in France.) After the declaration of war, he disappeared from Montparnasse. The police found him in the vineyards near Montpellier during the harvest season, with a basket of ripe grapes in his arms: this time, putting handcuffs on his wrists was not difficult. Whether Novsky escaped from France or was expelled is not known. We do know that he soon appeared in Berlin as one of the collaborators on the Social Democratic papers *Neue Zeitung* and *Leipziger Volkzeitung* under the pseudonyms B. N. Dolsky, Parabellum, Victor Tverdohlebov, Proletarsky, and N. L. Davidovich, and that, among other things, he wrote a famous review of Max Schippel's *The History of the Production of Sugar.* "He was," writes the Austrian Socialist Oscar Blum, "a strange mixture of amorality, cynicism, and spontaneous enthusiasm for ideas, books, music, and human beings. He looked, I'd say, like a cross between a professor and a bandit. But his intellectual *brio* was unquestionable. That virtuoso of Bolshevik journalism knew how to conduct conversations which were as full of explosives as his editorials." (The word "explosives" leads us to the bold conclusion that Oscar Blum might have been acquainted with the secret life of Novsky. Unless it is only a matter of inadvertent metaphor.) In Berlin at the outbreak of war, when the workers who rallied to the flag resembled ghosts, and cabarets full of thick cigar smoke resounded with female shrieks, and all that cannon fodder tried to drown its fears and despair in beer and schnapps, Novsky, Blum adds, was the only one who didn't lose his head in this European madhouse, the only one with a clear perspective.

On a bright autumn day, while lunching at the salon of the famous Davos Sanatorium in Basel, where he was undergoing treatment for his nerves and his slightly tubercular lungs, Novsky was visited by one of the members of the International named Levin. Dr. Grünwald approached them; he was Swiss, a disciple and friend of Jung, an authority in his field. According to Levin's testimony, the conversation was about the weather (the sunny October), about music (a recent concert given by a woman patient), about death (her musical soul had expired the night before). Between the meat and quince compote, served them by a waiter wearing a uniform and white gloves, Dr. Grünwald, losing the thread of the conversation, said in his nasal voice (only to fill an awkward silence): "There's some kind of revolution in St. Petersburg." (A pause.) The spoon in Levin's hand stopped in mid-air; Novsky started, and reached for his cigar. Dr. Grünwald felt a certain uneasiness. Trying to infuse his voice with absolute indifference, Novsky attempted to calm his trembling hands. "Excuse me. Where did you hear that?" As if apologizing, Dr. Grünwald said that he had seen the news that morning posted in the windows of the telegraph bureau in town. Without waiting for coffee, deathly pale, Novsky and Levin quickly left the salon and went into town by taxi. "I heard as if dazed," writes Levin, "the murmur coming from the salon, accompanied by the din of silver utensils like the tinkling of bells, and saw as through a fog the world we had left behind, and which was irretrievably sinking into the past, as into murky water."

Some documents lead us to conclude that Novsky, swept away by a wave of nationalism and bitterness, received the news of the truce, in spite of everything, as a blow. Levin speaks of a nervous crisis, and Meisnerova passes over this period with the haste of an accomplice. It seems, however, that without great resistance Novsky dropped his Mauser and, as a sign of remorse, burned the plans of his assault bombs and his 70-meter flame throwers, and joined the ranks of the Internationalists. Soon we find him, tireless and ubiquitous, among the supporters of the Brest-Litovsk peace, distributing antiwar propaganda leaflets, and, as a fiery agitator among the soldiers, standing on boxes of artillery shells, erect as a statue. In this quick and, so to speak, painless transformation of Novsky, a certain woman appears to have played a major role. In the chronicles of the Revolution, her name is recorded: Zinaida Mihailovna Maysner. A certain Leo Mikulin, who had the misfortune of falling in love with her, has portrayed her with words that could easily have been engraved on marble: "Nature gave her everything: intelligence, talent, beauty."

In February 1918, we see him in the wheat fields of Tula, Tambov, and Orel, on the banks of the Volga, in Kharkov, where under his supervision convoys of confiscated wheat were sent up to Moscow. In the black leather uniform of a commissar, with shiny boots, and a leather and sheepskin cap without insignia, he dispatched the convoys, his hand on his Mauser, until the last boat disappeared into the hazy distance. In May of the following year, he put on a camou-

flaged uniform and became a sharpshooter cutting off
Denikin's rear guard. The terrifying explosions in the south-
west sector of the front, taking place suddenly and mysteriously, leaving a slaughterhouse behind them, bore Novsky's
stamp just as handwriting can reveal character to an expert.
In late September, on the torpedo boat *Spartacus,* which flew
the red flag, Novsky set off for Reval on patrol. Suddenly
the boat ran into a strong British squadron of seven light
vessels armed with 25-millimeter guns. The torpedo boat
swerved and, with a reckless maneuver under the cloak of
the descending night, succeeded in reaching Kronstadt. If we
can believe the testimony of Captain Olimsky, the crew of
the torpedo boat should have been much more grateful for
their lucky rescue to the shrewdness of a woman, Zinaida
Mihailovna Maysner, than to Novsky's presence: she was the
one who negotiated by signal flag with the British flagship.

A letter from those years, written in Novsky's hand,
remains the only authentic document that combines, deeply
and mysteriously, revolutionary passion with sensual love:
"...As soon as I entered the university I found myself in
prison. I was arrested exactly thirteen times. Of the twelve
years that followed my first arrest, I spent more than half at
hard labor. In addition, three times I walked the painful road
of exile, a road that took three years of my life. During the
brief periods of my 'freedom' I watched, as in a movie
theater, the passing of sad Russian villages, towns, people,
and events, but I was always in flight—on a horse, on a boat,
in a cart. I never slept in the same bed for more than a month.
I've come to know the horror of Russian reality in the long
tedious winter evenings when the pale lights of Vasilevsky
Island barely blink, and a Russian village emerges in the
moonlight in a false and deceptive beauty. My only passion

was this arduous, rapturous, and mysterious profession of revolutionary.... Forgive me, Zina, and carry me in your heart; it will be as painful as a kidney stone."

The wedding ceremony was performed on December 27, 1919, on the torpedo boat *Spartacus,* which was anchored in Kronstadt harbor. The documents are few and contradictory. According to some, Zinaida Mihailovna was deathly pale, with "the pallor that unites death and beauty" (Mikulin), and looked more like an anarchist before a firing squad than the muse of the Revolution who has just escaped death by a hairbreadth. Mikulin mentions a white wedding wreath on Zinaida's hair, the sole symbol of old times and custom, while in his memoirs Olimsky talks about the white gauze which "like a wedding wreath" was wrapped around Maysner's wounded head. The same Olimsky, who proved more objective in his memory than the lyrical Mikulin (who passed Novsky by in silence, so to speak), gives an altogether schematic picture of the political commissar in that intimate moment: "Handsome, with a stern look, dressed monastically even for that solemn occasion, he appeared more like a young German student who had emerged the victor in a duel than a political commissar who had just come back from a fiery skirmish." Everyone more or less agrees in other details. The boat was quickly decorated with signal flags and lit up with red, green, and blue bulbs. Simultaneously celebrating the wedding and their victory over death, the crew appeared on deck freshly shaved and pink-cheeked, fully armed, as if for an inspection. But the cables informing the general staff about the course of the operation and the lucky rescue had drawn the attention of the officers of the Red fleet, who now arrived in blue military overcoats over their white summer uniforms. The

torpedo boat greeted them with whistles and the cheers of
the crew. The breathless radioman brought to the commander's bridge, where the young married couple had taken
shelter, uncoded cables with congratulations from all the
Soviet ports from Astrakhan to Enzeli: "Long live the newly-
weds!" "Long live the Red fleet!" "Hurrah for the brave
crew of the *Spartacus!*" The Revolutionary Council of Kronstadt sent armored cars with nine cases of French champagne
seized from the anarchists the day before. Kronstadt's brass
band climbed up the gangplank and onto the deck playing
marches. Because of the temperature, 22° below zero (Fahrenheit), the instruments had a strange, cracked sound, as if
made of ice. Patrol boats swarmed around, greeting the crew
with signals. Three times stern trios of Chekists came on deck,
their guns drawn, demanding that the celebration be stopped
for security reasons; three times they returned their guns to
their holsters at the mention of Novsky's name, and joined
the officers' chorus in its shouts of "Bitter! Bitter! . . . Sweet!
Sweet!" The empty champagne bottles flew over the sides like
25-millimeter artillery shells. At dawn, when the sun broke
through the fog of the winter morning like the flame of a
distant fire, one drunken Chekist saluted the birth of the new
day with a salvo from the antiaircraft gun. The crew was
strewn all over the deck as if dead, lying on heaps of broken
glass, empty bottles, confetti, and small frozen puddles of
French champagne rosy as blood. (The reader recognizes,
surely, the awkward lyricism of Leo Mikulin, a student of
the Imagists.)

   This marriage was dissolved after eighteen months, and
Zinaida Mihailovna, during an illegal excursion to Europe,
became the companion of the Soviet diplomat A. D. Kara-
mazov. As far as her brief marriage to Novsky is concerned,

some documents tell of tormented scenes of jealousy and passionate reconciliations. The claim that Novsky used to whip Zinaida Mihailovna in his jealous fits, however, may well be the fruit of another jealous imagination—that of Mikulin. In her autobiographical book *Wave After Wave,* Zinaida Mihailovna passes over her personal memories as if writing them on water: the whip appears here only in its historical and metaphorical context as the "knout" that mercilessly whips the face of the Russian people.

(Zinaida Mihailovna Maysner died of malaria in August 1926. In Persia. She was not quite thirty years old.)

As we have mentioned before, it is impossible to establish the exact chronology of Novsky's life during the civil war years and those immediately following. It is known that in 1920 he fought against the rebellious and despotic emirs in Turkestan, and subjugated them with their own weapons of cunning and cruelty; that during the hot summer of 1921, noted in the annals for the invasion of malarial mosquitoes and horseflies that swarmed down to suck the people's blood, he was in charge of the liquidation of banditry in the Tambov Region, on which occasion he received a saber or knife wound that gave his face the cruel stamp of heroism. At the Congress of Eastern Peoples we find him at the presidential table, aloof, with the perennial cigarette between his yellowed teeth. His speech was greeted with applause, but one reporter observed the absence of zeal, and the dull gaze of this man whom they had once called "the Bolshevik Hamlet." We know also that for a time he served as the political commissar of the Caucasus-Caspian Revolutionary Naval Committee, and that he was an artillery corps officer in the Red Army, then a diplomat in Afghanistan and Estonia. At the

end of 1924 he appeared in London as a member of the
delegation negotiating with the perpetually distrustful British. On that occasion he personally initiated contact with
representatives of the trade unions, who invited him to the
next congress in Hull.

As far as we know, he held his last position in Kazakhstan, in the Central Office for Communications and Liaisons.
He was bored; and in his office he again began to draw plans
and make calculations: a bomb the size of a walnut, with
tremendous destructive power, obsessed him until the end of
his life.

B. D. Novsky, the representative of the People's Commissariat for Communications and Liaisons, was arrested in
Kazakhstan on December 23, 1930, at two o'clock in the
morning. His arrest was much less dramatic than reported in
the West. According to the reliable testimony of his sister,
there was no armed resistance and fighting on the stairs.
Novsky was asked urgently over the telephone to come to
the Central Office. The voice was probably that of the engineer on duty: Butenko. During the search, which lasted until
eight o'clock in the morning, all his documents, photographs,
manuscripts, sketches, and plans, as well as his books, were
taken. This was the first step toward the liquidation of
Novsky. On the basis of very recent information, given by
A. L. Rubina, Novsky's sister, this is what happened later:

Novsky was confronted with a certain Reinhold, T. S.
Reinhold, who confessed that he was a British spy, and that
by order he had been sabotaging the economy. Novsky maintained that he had never before seen this unfortunate man
with a cracked voice and a dull gaze. After fifteen days,
which were granted to Novsky to think things over, he was

again brought before the interrogator, and offered sand-
wiches and a cigarette. Novsky refused the offer and asked
for a pencil and paper, to get in touch with some people in
high places. At dawn the next day he was taken out of his
cell and sent to Suzdal. When the car arrived at the railroad
station on that icy morning, the platform was deserted. A
single cattle car stood on a siding, and it was to this car that
they took Novsky. Fedukin, the tall, pock-marked, and un-
bending interrogator, spent some five hours alone with
Novsky in this cattle car (the doors were locked from the
outside), trying to persuade him of the moral obligation of
making a false confession. These negotiations failed entirely.
Then followed long nights without days spent in solitary
confinement in Suzdal Prison, in a damp stone-walled cell
known as the "doghouse," which had the major architectural
advantage of making a man feel as if he were buried alive,
so that he experienced his mortal being, in comparison with
the eternity of stone and time, as a speck of dust in the ocean
of timelessness. Novsky was already a man of failing health;
the long years of hard labor and revolutionary zeal, which
feeds on blood and glands, had weakened his lungs, kidneys,
and joints. His body was now covered with boils, which
would burst under the blows of rubber truncheons, oozing
out his precious blood along with useless pus. Nevertheless,
it seems that in contact with the stone of his living tomb,
Novsky drew some metaphysical conclusions undoubtedly
not much different from those suggesting the thought that
man is only a speck of dust in the ocean of timelessness; but
this also revealed to him another conclusion, which the
architects of the "doghouse" could not have foreseen: nothing
for nothing. The man who found in his heart this heretical
and dangerous thought, which speaks of the futility of one's
own being-in-time, finds himself, however, faced with another

(final) dilemma: whether to accept the transitoriness of this being-in-time for the sake of that precious and expensively acquired knowledge (which excludes any morality and therefore is made in absolute freedom), or, for the sake of that same knowledge, to yield oneself to the embrace of nothingness.

For Fedukin it was a question of honor, the greatest challenge: to break down Novsky. In his long career as an interrogator, he had always succeeded: in breaking their backs, he had also broken the wills of even the most tenacious prisoners (which was why they always gave him the toughest material). Novsky, however, stood before him like a scientific puzzle, an unknown organism that behaved quite unpredictably and atypically in relation to Fedukin's entire experience. (There is no doubt that in Fedukin's laudable theorizing there was no bookishness, given his less than modest education, so that any connection with teleological reasoning would have escaped him. He must have felt like the originator of a doctrine, which he formulated very simply, to make it comprehensible to any man: "Even a stone would talk if you broke its teeth.")*

* The journal *Worker* published several fragments from Fedukin's memoirs, called *The Second Front* (August and November 1964). Thus far, this autobiographical "piece" covers only the earliest period of Fedukin's "background activity," but judging by this material, in which the vividness of his actual practice is replaced by overly schematic reflections, I am afraid that even the complete edition of his memoirs would not reveal the secret of his genius: it seems to me that, except in actual practice, Fedukin was a theoretical zero. He extracted confessions according to the most profound principles of inner psychology without even being aware that psychology existed; he dealt with human souls and their secrets without knowing that he did. But even now, what really attracts us in Fedukin's remembrances are his descriptions of nature: the austere beauty of the Siberian landscape, the sunrise over the frozen tundra, diluvial rains and treacherous waters cutting through the taiga, the silence of distant lakes, their steel color—all of which testifies to his undeniable literary talent.

On the night of January 28–29, they led from his cell a man who still bore the name Novsky, though he was now only the empty shell of a being, a heap of decayed and ever-tortured flesh. In Novsky's dull gaze one could read, as the only sign of soul and life, the decision to endure, to write the last page of his biography according to his own will and fully conscious, as one writes a last testament. He formulated his thought like this: "I've reached my mature years—why spoil my biography?" He therefore seemed to have realized that even this last trial was not only the final page of the autobiography which he had been consciously writing with his blood and brain for some forty years, but also that this was indeed the sum of his living, the conclusion on which everything hinged, and all the rest was (and had been) only a minor treatise, the arithmetical calculation whose value was insignificant in relation to the final formula that gave meaning to these subordinate operations.

Novsky was led out of the cell by two guards, who supported him on each side, down some half-dark stairs that wound vertiginously into the depths of the triple cellar of the prison. They brought him to a room illuminated by a bare light bulb that hung from the ceiling. The guards released him, and Novsky staggered. He heard the iron door close behind him, but at first he noticed only the light, which cut painfully into his consciousness. The door opened again, and the same two guards, preceded by Fedukin, brought in a young man and left him about one meter from Novsky. It flashed through Novsky's mind that this was probably another false confrontation, one of many, so he stubbornly clenched his toothless jaws and with a painful effort opened his swollen eyelids to get a look at the young man. He expected to see again a corpse with dull eyes (like Reinhold), but with a shiver very much like foreboding he saw before him young, living eyes full of fear that was human, altogether human. The young man was naked to the waist; with astonishment and the dread of the unknown, Novsky realized that his muscular body was entirely devoid of blue marks, without a single bruise, with healthy dark skin untouched yet by putrefaction. But what astonished and frightened him the most was that gaze, whose meaning he could not penetrate, that unknown game into which he was being drawn, at the point when he thought that everything was already over in the best possible sense. Could he have fathomed what the ingenious and infernal intuition of Fedukin was preparing for him? Fedukin was standing behind him, invisible yet present, holding his breath, letting Novsky discover it for himself and be horrified by it and then, when the denial born of terror whispered to him that *that* was impossible, ready to hit him suddenly with the truth, the truth more awful than the merciful bullet he could use to blow his brains out.

At the same moment that the denial born of terror whispered to Novsky that *that* was impossible, he heard Fedukin's voice: "If Novsky doesn't confess, we'll kill you!" The young man's face grew distorted with fear, and he fell on his knees in front of Novsky. Novsky shut his eyes, but because of the handcuffs couldn't cover his ears so as not to hear the young man's pleadings, which suddenly, as if by some miracle, began to shake the hard rock of his resolution, to break down his will. The young man was imploring him with a trembling, broken voice to confess for the sake of his life. Novsky clearly heard the guards cock their guns. Behind his tightly shut lids there arose in him, simultaneously with the reawakening of pain and the premonition of failure, hatred; he had enough time to realize that Fedukin had seen through him and had decided to devastate him where he felt the strongest: in his egocentricity. For if Novsky had discovered the saving but dangerous idea of the futility of one's own being-in-time and suffering, this was still a moral choice; Fedukin's intuitive genius had sensed that this choice does not exclude morality—quite the contrary. The guns must have had silencers, since Novsky hardly heard the shots. When he opened his eyes, the young man was lying in front of him in a pool of blood, his brains spilled out.

Fedukin didn't waste words. He knew that Novsky had understood; he signaled to the guards to take Novsky away, and they lifted him up by the arms. Fedukin gave him twenty-four hours to think it over in his well-guarded cell, where again he would be able, "under the death shroud of stone,"* to ascertain his moral position, which was whispering demoniacally into his ear that his biography was final and well rounded, without flaws, as perfect as a sculpture. The next night, that of January 29–30, the scene was repeated: the guards led Novsky down the vertiginous spiral stairs into the deep cellars of the prison. Novsky realized with horror that this repetition was not accidental, but part of an infernal plan: each day of his life would be paid for with the life of another man; the perfection of his biography would be destroyed, his life work (his life) deformed by these final pages.

Fedukin's direction was perfect: the *mise en scène* of the previous night was the same, with the same Fedukin, the same cellar, the same light bulb, the same Novsky—the elements entirely sufficient to give the repeated action the appearance of something identical and inevitable, as the

* The expression was used by Leo Mikulin to immortalize his own biography, sometime in 1936. This metaphor is less arbitrary than it seems at first glance; Mikulin died of a heart attack in solitary confinement in Suzdal Prison. (Some sources maintain that he was strangled.)

alteration of day and night is inevitable. Only this half-naked young man trembling in front of him was slightly different (only as one day spent in the same cell differs from another). Fedukin probably sensed, by the silence that fell for a moment, how much harder today's trial was for Novsky than yesterday's; today, while Novsky stood eye to eye with the unknown young man, there remained not even a shred of hope for his morality, no taking of shelter in some thought that could come to his rescue, a thought that could whisper to him, despite certain clear outside indications, that this was *impossible:* last night's quick and efficient demonstration had shown him the futility of this kind of thought, that such a thought was deadly. (And tomorrow, and the day after tomorrow, and in three or ten days more, this thought would become even more absurd, even more impossible.)

Novsky thought that he knew this young man from somewhere. He had fair skin sprinkled with freckles, an unhealthy complexion, thick dark hair, and slightly crossed eyes; most likely he wore glasses, and it seemed to Novsky that he could even discern their marks still fresh on the bridge of his nose. The thought that this young man actually looked like himself some twenty years ago struck him as absurd, and he tried to discard it; nevertheless, for a split second he couldn't help thinking that this resemblance (if real and purposeful) carried a certain risk for Fedukin's interrogation, and could be regarded in some way as an error and a crack in Fedukin's direction. But Fedukin must have sensed, too, that if this resemblance was purposeful and the result of his careful selection, then this notion of resemblance, of identity, would inevitably lead Novsky to realize the major difference: this resemblance would show him that he was killing men similar to himself, men whose role carried the seed of a future biography, consistent, well rounded, much like his own, but destroyed at the very onset, nipped in the bud, so to speak, by his own doing. By his stubborn refusal to co-operate with the inquiry, he would find himself (indeed, he already did) at the beginning of a long series of murders committed in his name.

Novsky felt the presence of Fedukin behind him, hold-ing his breath and waiting in ambush for his thoughts, his decision, just as he felt the presence of the guards, who stood to one side with cocked guns, ready to commit murder *by his hand*. Fedukin's voice was calm, unthreatening, as if delivering the result of an entirely logical operation: "You'll die, Isaievich, if Novsky doesn't confess." Before Novsky had a chance to say anything at all, before he had a chance to think of the shameful conditions of his surrender, the young man sized him up with his nearsighted eyes, moved close to his face, and whispered to him in a voice that made Novsky shudder: "Boris Davidovich, don't let the sons of bitches get you!"

In that same instant two shots resounded almost simul-taneously, though barely audible, as when a cork pops out of a champagne bottle. He could not help opening his tightly shut lids to verify his crime: again the guards had shot point-blank into the back of the neck, their barrels aimed up toward the skull; the young man's face was unrecognizable.

Fedukin left the cellar without a word and the guards took Novsky away and threw him on the stone floor. Novsky spent nightmarish hours in his cell, surrounded by rats.

The next evening, after the third shift of guards came on, he asked to see the interrogator.

That same night they transferred him from the stone cell to the prison hospital, where he spent some ten days, as if in a coma, under the watchful eyes of guards and hospital personnel, who were given the assignment of rebuilding out of these remnants a man worthy of that name. Fedukin knew from experience that men far less tough than Novsky became infused with an unsuspected strength when the moment beyond all limits was reached, and when the only issue was to die honorably: at the moment of dying they tried to derive from death the greatest possible gain by an obstinate resolution, which, perhaps because of physical exhaustion, was most often reduced to heroic silence. Practice had also taught him that the restored functioning of the organism, normal blood circulation and the absence of pain, gave convalescents and former death candidates a certain organic conformity, which caused as a consequence, paradoxical as it seems, the weakening of the will and the ever-decreasing need for heroic bravado.

In the meantime, the accusation that Novsky had belonged to a spy network for the British was dropped, especially after the unsuccessful confrontation with Reinhold. (British trade unions contributed greatly to this, by making a loud noise in the European press about Novsky's arrest and by denouncing as entirely unfounded and absurd accusations that appeared in the official press: the rendezvous in Berlin with a certain Richards, who had allegedly bribed Novsky, like Judas, with thirty pieces of silver, was refuted by the perfect alibi of the said Richards: on that day he was attending the trade union conference in Hull.) This awkward intervention by the trade unions placed before the investigators the none-too-easy task of proving the accuracy of their claims, in order to save their reputation on a much wider international plane.

The negotiations lasted from February 8 to 21. Novsky

prolonged the inquiry, trying to incorporate into the confession—probably the only document of his that would remain after his death—a certain wording that would not only cushion his final downfall but also whisper to a future investigator, through the skillfully woven contradictions and exaggerations, that the whole structure of this confession rested on a lie squeezed out of him by torture. This was why he fought with unsuspected strength for every word, every phrase. For his part, Fedukin, no less resolute and cautious, made maximal demands. Through long nights the two men struggled over the difficult text of the confession, panting and exhausted, their heads bent over the pages enveloped in the thick cigarette smoke, each trying to incorporate into it some of his own passion, his own beliefs, his own outlook from a higher perspective. Fedukin knew just as well as Novsky (and let him know it) that all this—the entire text of the confession, formulated on ten closely typed pages— was pure fiction, which he alone, Fedukin, had concocted during the long hours of the night, typing with two fingers, awkwardly and slowly (he liked to do everything himself), trying to draw logical conclusions from certain assumptions. He was therefore not interested in the so-called facts or characters, but in those assumptions and their logical use; in the final analysis his reasons were the same as Novsky's, when Novsky, starting from another premise, ideal and idealized, rejected any assumption beforehand. Lastly, I believe that both acted from reasons that transcended narrow egocentric goals: Novsky fought to preserve in his death and downfall the dignity of not only his own image but also that of all revolutionaries, while Fedukin, in his search for fiction and premises, strove to preserve the sternness and consistency of revolutionary justice and of those who dispense this justice;

for it was better that the so-called truth of a single man, one tiny organism, be destroyed than that higher interests and principles be questioned. If, in the later stages of interrogation, Fedukin lunged at his obstinate victims, this was not the whim of a neurotic or a cocaine addict, as some believe, but a struggle for his convictions which, like his victims', he considered to be altruistic, inviolable, and sacred. What provoked Fedukin's fury and dedicated hatred was precisely this sentimental egocentricity of the accused, their pathological need to prove their own *innocence*, their own little *truths*, this neurotic going around in circles of so-called facts encompassed by the meridians of their skulls. It enraged him that this blind truth of theirs could not be incorporated into a system of higher value, a higher justice which demanded sacrifice, and which did not and must not care about human weakness. This was why for Fedukin anyone became a blood enemy who could not comprehend this simple and almost obvious fact: to sign a confession *for the sake of duty* was not only a logical but also a moral act, and therefore worthy of respect. Novsky's case was all the more defeating for him since he respected Novsky as a revolutionary and, for a period of time some ten years ago, had regarded him as a model. That day in the cattle car on the siding of the Suzdal railroad station, he had, despite everything, approached him with due respect for his person and in full confidence. Since then, however, he had experienced a disillusionment that had entirely destroyed in his eyes the myth of a revolutionary: Novsky could not understand that his own egocentricity (surely a product of flattery and praise) was stronger in him than his sense of duty.

One early morning in late February, Novsky returned to his cell, exhausted but satisfied, ready to memorize the revised manuscript of his confession. The manuscript was edited, with corrections scribbled over it in ink as red as blood; his confession seemed to him so weighty that he could not escape the death sentence. He smiled, or it seemed to him that he was smiling. Fedukin had accomplished his secret intention of preparing the final chapter of his honorable biography. Under the cold ashes of these absurd accusations, future investigators would discover the pathos of a life and the consistent ending (despite everything) of a perfect biography.

So the indictment was finally revised on February 27, and the trial for the saboteurs scheduled for the middle of March. At the beginning of May, after a long postponement, there was a sudden and unexpected change in the plans of the investigation. Novsky was brought into Fedukin's office for the last rehearsal of his memorized confession. Fedukin informed him that the indictment had been altered, and handed him the typewritten text of the new one. Standing between the two guards, Novsky read the text and suddenly began howling, or so it seemed to him. They dragged him again to the "doghouse" and left him there among the well-fed rats. Novsky tried to smash his head against the stone wall of the cell; they put him in a straitjacket and took him to a hospital room. Awaking from the delirium induced by morphine injections, Novsky asked to see the interrogator.

In the meantime, Fedukin, conducting two interrogations simultaneously, succeeded in getting a confession out of a certain Paresyan, who, influenced only by threats (and most likely a drink or two), signed a statement in which he claimed that he personally had delivered the first sum of money to Novsky as early as May 1925, when they were co-workers in the cable factory in Novosibirsk. That money,

Paresyan claimed, was a part of the regular trimonthly sum they received from Berlin as a bribe for the satisfactory arrangements that Novsky, through Paresyan and a man named Titelheim, was setting up for certain foreign firms, primarily German and British. Titelheim, an engineer with a small goatee and glasses, a man of the old school with old-fashioned principles, couldn't understand why he had to drag into his confession other people whom he didn't even know, but Fedukin found a way to persuade him: after a long resistance old Titelheim, determined to die honorably, heard terrible screams from the adjoining room, and recognized the voice of his only daughter. Promised that her life would be spared, he agreed to all of Fedukin's conditions, and signed the statement without even reading it. (Years went by before the truth about the Titelheims came to light: in some transit labor camp the old man found out almost by chance, from a woman prisoner named Ginsburg, that his daughter had been murdered in a prison cell on the very day of his interrogation.)

In the middle of May the confrontation between those two and Novsky took place. It seemed to Novsky that Paresyan reeked of vodka; with a thick tongue he threw at Novsky in bad Russian the fantastic details of their long-standing collaboration. From Paresyan's sincere fury, Novsky knew that Fedukin, in his art of squeezing out confessions, had in Paresyan's case attained that ideal level of cooperation which was the goal of every decent interrogation: Paresyan, thanks to Fedukin's creative genius, had accepted the premises as the living reality, more real than a jumble of facts, and had colored those premises with his own remorse and hatred. Titelheim, oblivious, with a gaze turned toward a distant dead world, couldn't remember the details he had

put in the signed statement, and Fedukin had to remind him
sternly of the rules of good conduct. Titelheim slowly remembered the amount, cited figures, places, and dates.
Novsky realized that his last chance for rescue was slipping
away, that Fedukin had prepared the most dishonorable of
deaths for him: he would die as a thief who, like Judas, had
sold his soul for thirty pieces of silver. (Most likely it will
remain forever a secret whether this was only a part of
Fedukin's prepared plan to get Novsky to cooperate sincerely, or yet another revision of the indictment brought
about by the one who didn't want to die dishonorably.)

That night, after the confrontation, Novsky again tried
to commit suicide and thereby save a part of the legend. The
watchful eye and doglike hearing of the guards, however,
detected some suspicious sound, probably the sigh of relief
that reached them from the dying man's cell: with his veins
slashed, Novsky was taken to the hospital cell, where he
stubbornly kept tearing off the bandages, and they had to
feed him intravenously. (This was the next step toward the
final liquidation of Novsky.)

In the face of such obstinacy, Fedukin gave in and
named Novsky (on the basis of the previous indictment) as
the leader of the conspiracy. Confronted separately with
each member of the alleged sabotage cell (which was being
assembled under Fedukin's supervision), Novsky, staring
into space with dead, astigmatic eyes, recognized in some of
the frightened strangers those with whom "he had been
hatching brave plots to blow up installations that were of
vital importance to the military industry." Along with this
he added certain details from the memorized script. Fedukin,
who had finally discovered in Novsky a useful and skillful
collaborator, left it to Novsky's own intelligence to smooth
out some contradictions and inconsistencies in the complex

script of the indictment. (In this, Novsky used his lifelong experience, acquired in the Czar's prisons and in fights against cautious procurators.)

The quiet course of this collaboration was marred only once, in late May, when Novsky was confronted with a certain Rabinovich. I. I. Rabinovich had been Novsky's spiritual mentor since the early Pavlograd days; he was an expert engineer, who had discovered talent in Novsky and initiated him into the secrets of making explosives. In the course of Novsky's irregular but no less brilliant studies, the role of Isaac Rabinovich had been manifold: not only had he supplied young Novsky with advice and professional literature, but also on many occasions he had, by his reputation and intervention, come to his rescue, putting up high bail for him, etc. (The fearful results of certain explosions that shook St. Petersburg around 1910 had provoked justified suspicions in old Rabinovich, and for a time had alienated him from his overly talented student.) For the many favors he had obtained from him, Novsky had repaid Rabinovich during the civil war, when he pulled him out of the clutches of zealous Chekists, who saw in Rabinovich a would-be assassin and harbored a profound distrust of him, inspired by his knowledge of explosives. It seems, though, that the bond between Novsky and Rabinovich was primarily one of affection: the old story of the idealized father, and that father's discovery of his secret dreams in a young man in whom he recognized his own traits. Consequently, Novsky refused to sign the part of the indictment that referred to Rabinovich. (The presence of Rabinovich in the courtroom, however, was of primary importance for the interrogation, because of his profile: heredity, race, environment.) Thereupon Fedukin played his last card: he pulled out of his desk drawer Paresyan's and Titelheim's confessions, which in the meantime had been enriched by new details, and by the confessions of three additional participants in what was called "the Great Theft of Public Funds." All three named Novsky as the ringleader and gave details about his character, reducing his revolutionary élan to an unscrupulous lust for money, and his legendary asceticism to a comical mask and to shrewdness. Some documents touched on the early Paris and St. Petersburg days, with clear allusions to the fashionable life of the young revolutionary, who undoubtedly bought his famous hats and red vests with money received from the fat funds of the Okhrana.

Novsky realized that he had no choice. In exchange for a return favor from Fedukin, he signed the confession to the effect that Professor Rabinovich had collaborated with him in the making of explosives. The details concerning the kind of shrapnel and detonator; the destructive power of the gunpowder, dynamite, kerosene, and TNT; the method of construction, and place where the infernal machines were made, as well as their destructive power under particular conditions —all this Novsky himself dictated into the statement. In exchange, in front of Novsky, Fedukin burned in a big iron stove the compromising document (now useless) about the group of thieves and speculators.

In the middle of April, the trial of the saboteurs, now involving twenty members, was conducted behind closed doors. According to the testimony of a certain Snaserov, Novsky, despite his occasional obliviousness, spoke with a passion that Snaserov attributed to high fever. "It was his best political speech yet," he adds, not without malice (clearly alluding to those false rumors that Novsky was a poor speaker: the first premature sign of the destruction of the myth known as Novsky.) Another survivor of this trial, Kaurin, gives him credit, stating that, despite the horrendous torture to which he had been subjected during the many months of his interrogation, he did not lose any of his sharpness, "which overwhelmed us all." He also says: "Once he was an agile man with quick, lively eyes, and now he drags his feet, he is gaunt, his eyes deep in their sockets, and at times he seems totally absent; he looks like a ghost, but not his own. At least not until he speaks; then again he is more a devil than a man." It should be pointed out, however, that Novsky's role in this trial was greatly determined by the trade unions and the émigré press, which insisted that in the framework of this trial lurked hidden provocateurs who had nothing to do with revolutionaries. Therefore Novsky aimed the deadly power of his eloquence in that direction, trying in a fit of honest fury to demolish these arguments of the Mensheviks and the trade unions, which could reduce his biography and his end to that which he feared the most, and against which, all these months, he had fought a bloody battle to the death.

The state prosecutor, V. N. Krichenko, an expert on high treason, asked the highest punishment for the first five men indicted, but, to general astonishment, as Kaurin says, in his closing speech Krichenko did not "drag Novsky through the mud." (I tend to believe that the role of Novsky in this trial was bought at that price.) In a way he even gave Novsky credit, since Novsky was able to retain his integrity until the very end, in spite of everything (as proved by his sincere cooperation with the interrogation). Krichenko even called him an "old revolutionary," stressing the fact that Novsky had always been a fanatic in his ideas and convictions, which in one fatal moment he had placed in the service of the counterrevolution and the international bourgeois conspiracy. Striving to find a scientific explanation for this moral deviation, Krichenko discovered it in the petit-bourgeois background of the accused, and in the destructive influence of his frequent visits to the West, during which he was more interested in literary trivia than in politics. In the Kolyma hospital, where he was lying half blind and sick with scurvy, old Rabinovich told Dr. Taube about the meeting that took place after the trial between himself and Novsky in the anteroom of the court. "Boris Davidovich," he had said to Novsky, "I'm afraid that you must be out of your mind. You'll bury us all with your plea." Novsky answered him with a strange expression on his face, which seemed to be the shadow of a smile. "Isaac Ilich, you should know the Jewish funeral custom: at the moment when they are ready to take the corpse from the synagogue to the cemetery, one servant of Yahweh bends over the deceased, calls him by name, and says in a loud voice: 'Know that you are dead!'" He paused a moment, then added: "An excellent custom!"

As a sign of gratitude—and probably convinced that he had got out of death the most a living man could—Novsky insisted in his final speech that his crimes fully deserved the death sentence as the only just punishment, that he did not find the decision of the prosecutor too severe, and would not appeal the case to save his life. Since he managed to avoid the noose of the shameful gallows, he considered death before a firing squad a happy and fitting ending; even outside this moral context, he must have felt that some higher justice demanded that he die by steel and lead.

But they did not kill him (it is more difficult, it seems, to choose death than life): the sentence was reduced, and after one year in the shadow of death, he embarked again on the hard road of exile. At the beginning of 1934, under the name Dolsky—the same one he had adopted during his last imprisonment under the Czar—we find him in the recently colonized Turgay. (One should not try to find in his change of names a message for the future, a sign of defiance and provocation, for Novsky was guided primarily by practical considerations: some of his documents still bore that name.) The same year he received permission from the government to settle in the even more remote Aktyubinsk, where, surrounded by suspicious colonists, he worked on a farm growing sugar beets. In December, his sister was granted permission to visit him, and found him ill: Novsky complained of pains in his kidneys. By this time he had permanent dentures made of stainless steel. (Whether his teeth were broken during the interrogation, as Dr. Taube maintained, is difficult to say.) Novsky refused her suggestion that she try to obtain permission for his transfer to Moscow: he did not want to look the world in the eye. "He expected death during the early morning hours," she writes, "which coincided with those of his arrest: his body rigid, glassy-eyed, he'd stare in the direction of the door, which even so he never locked. When three o'clock had passed, he'd pick up his guitar and softly sing entirely unintelligible songs. He had auditory hallucinations and heard voices and footsteps in the hallway." (In those years the following anecdote made the rounds in Moscow: "What's our Novsky doing?" "He's drinking tea with currant jam and playing the 'International' on the guitar." "But with a mute," someone would add maliciously.)

It is known that Novsky was arrested again during the terrible winter of 1937 and taken somewhere. The next year we uncover his tracks in distant Insulma. The last letter written by him has the postmark of Kem, in the vicinity of the Solovetski Islands.

The continuation and the end of Novsky's history is based on Carl Fridrichovich (who mistakenly calls him

Podolsky, instead of Dolsky); the setting: the distant, icy North, Norilsk.

Novsky disappeared from the camp in a mysterious and inexplicable way, most likely during one of those awful storms when the tower guards, the firearms, and the German shepherds were equally helpless. After the storm had died down, the pursuers set off in search of the fugitive, relying on the bloodthirsty instinct of their dogs. For three days the camp inmates awaited in vain the command "Get out!"; for three days the furious foaming German shepherds struggled to wrest free from their steel collars, dragging the exhausted pursuers over deep snowdrifts. On the fourth day, a guard spotted Novsky at the ironworks, unshaven and looking like an apparition, warming himself next to the furnace. They released the German shepherds. Following the howls of the dogs, the pursuers burst into the foundry building. The fugitive was on the ladder at the top of the furnace, illuminated by the flames. One eager guard began to climb up. As the guard approached him, Novsky leaped into the boiling mass. The guards saw him disappear before their very eyes; he rose like a wisp of smoke, deaf to their commands, defiant, free from German shepherds, from cold, from heat, from punishment, and from remorse.

This brave man died on November 21, 1937, at four o'clock in the afternoon. He left a few cigarettes and a toothbrush.

In late June 1956, the London *Times,* which still seemed to believe in ghosts, announced that Novsky had been seen in Moscow near the Kremlin wall. He was recognized by his steel dentures. This news was carried by the entire Western bourgeois press, eager for intrigue and sensation.

DOGS AND BOOKS

FOR FILIP DAVID

In the year of Our Lord 1330, on the twenty-third day of the twelfth month, it came to the vigilant ears of the Most Venerable Father in Christ, Monsignor Jacques, by the grace of God Bishop of Pamiers, that Baruch David Neumann, a refugee from Germany and a former Jew, had abandoned the blindness and perfidy of Judaism and been converted to the Christian faith; that he had received the sacrament of holy baptism in the town of Toulouse at a time of persecution, at the instigation of the devout Pastoureaux; and that afterward, "like a dog who goggles his vomit," this Baruch David Neumann used the opportunity—since in the town of Pamiers he had lived like a Jew with other Jews—to return to that sect offensive to God, and to his former Jewish ways, so that His Excellency the Bishop ordered that he be arrested and thrown in the dungeon.

Finally, he ordered that he be brought to him, and Baruch Neumann appeared before him in the Bishop's great hall, the left wing of which opened onto the torture chamber.

Monsignor Jacques gave the order that Baruch be brought through this chamber to remind him of the instruments God has mercifully placed in our hands in the service of His Holy Faith and for the salvation of the human soul.

Monsignor Jacques had beside him at the table as his helper Friar Gaillard de Pamiers, the representative of the Inquisitor of Carcassonne. Also present were the Magistrate Bernard Faissasier of Pamiers and the Magistrate David de Troyes, a Jew who had been called in as interpreter to His Excellency the Bishop, in case Baruch was brazen enough to touch on dogma and the Law, since he was known to be a specialist in the Old Testament, Jewish Law, and the Book of the Evil One.*

---

* "The Book of the Evil One" is only one of the famous metaphors for the no-less-famous Talmud. In 1320 Pope John XXII had ordered that every copy of this heretical book be seized and burned at the stake. It is known that at that time throughout the entire Christian Archipelago soldiers at the customs barriers would search Jewish caravans, rummaging through smuggled merchandise—silks, leathers, and spices—while paying no attention to it (except out of personal greed), and that Saint Bernard dogs, with their talent for sniffing out "the writings of the Evil One," would sniff the greasy caftans of bearded merchants and put their muzzles under the skirts of frightened women. Finally the dogs caused a severe epidemic of rabies, and began also biting Christian merchants and putting their muzzles under the robes of innocent pilgrims, priests, and nuns who were smuggling dried fish and Camembert, commonly known as *crotte de diable* (devil's dung), out of Catalonia. Tracking down the Talmud, however, did not stop with this; in 1336 alone Jean Guy, called "*en fer*," "of Iron," seized and burned at the stake two cartloads of that incriminated book, while his earlier and later accomplishments unfortunately remain unknown to the present researchers. This Jean Guy of Iron, *en Fer* (some of his opponents, carried away by the associations of the sound of *en fer,* and by envy, pronounced and wrote as *Enfer,* meaning hell), showed himself much too zealous, it seems: along with the Talmud, he began to burn books not on the official Index of the Pope, and people too, so that for a period of time he was exposed to pressure from the clergy, who were mightily afraid of him, and who acted according to the Pope's, and God's, instructions. It is known that Jean Guy of Iron emerged from this bloody battle the victor, and that most of his opponents were burned at the stake. They say he died in his monastic cell half mad, surrounded by books and dogs.

Monsignor Jacques began, therefore, to question Baruch about all these things, since the Jew swore on Moses' Law that he would tell only the truth, primarily about himself but also about others, living and dead, whom he would call as witnesses.

When this came to pass, he said and confessed as follows:

This year (on last Thursday it was exactly a month) the devout Pastoureaux arrived in Grenade armed with long knives, spears, and whips, with crosses made out of goatskin sewn to their clothes, carrying rebel flags and threatening to exterminate all Jews. Solomon Vudas, a young Jew, then found the Grand Defender of Grenade in the company of his scribe, the Jew Eleazar, and asked him, as he told me later, whether he would protect him from the devout Pastoureaux. He said that he would. However, since the Pastoureaux kept arriving in ever-increasing numbers and began searching even the houses of Christians and prominent citizens, he told Solomon that he would not be able to protect him any longer, and advised him to take a boat down the Garonne to Verdun, to a larger and safer castle belonging to a friend. So Solomon took the boat and set off downstream toward Verdun. When the Pastoureaux saw him from the bank, they also got a boat and oars, pulled him out of the water, and, after tying him up, took him to Grenade, all the while telling him he must be either converted or killed. The Grand Defender, who was watching all this from the bank, his hand on his forehead, approached them and said that if they killed Solomon, it would be as if they cut off his own head. They answered that if this were so, they would carry out his wish. Solomon said he did not wish the judge to be hurt in any way because of him, and asked the Pastoureaux what they wanted of him. They repeated: he must

be either converted or killed. Solomon declared that he would
rather be converted. At once they baptized him in the murky
waters of the Garonne, along with Eleazar the scribe, since
they had with them a young priest who surely knew the
procedure. Two pious women sewed crosses of goatskin on
their clothes and then they were let go.

The next day Solomon and Eleazar came to see me in
Toulouse, told me all that had happened, and said that they
were converted, but not of their own free will; if they could,
they would like to revert to their own faith. They also said
that if one day Yahweh mercifully opened their eyes and
showed them that the new laws were better than the old,
that the soul sinned less toward man and beast in the fold of
the new faith, then they would convert of their own free
will, sincerely. I answered that I did not know what to
advise them; perhaps they could, I told them, return unpunished into the fold of Judaism if their souls were freed
from Christian laws, and that I would consult Friar Raymond
Leinach, assistant to His Excellency the Inquisitor of Toulouse, who would certainly be able to give them advice and
absolution. So together with Bonnet, a Jew from Agen, I
went to see Friar Raymond and the attorney Jacques
Marques, notary to His Excellency the Inquisitor of Toulouse.
I described the misfortune that had befallen Solomon, and
asked them whether the conversion of someone against his
will was licit, and whether faith accepted through naked
fear for one's life had any value. They told me that such a
conversion was illicit. I returned at once to Solomon and
Eleazar and brought them the message from Friar Raymond
and attorney Jacques that their conversion did not have the
force of true faith, and that they could return to the faith of
Moses. Solomon subsequently delivered his person into the
hands of Monsignor the Councillor of Toulouse, so that the

latter would obtain for him the opinion of the Roman Curia about the efficacy of this conversion, since Solomon feared that his return to Judaism could be interpreted as a sign of hypocrisy.

When all this was done, Solomon and Eleazar returned to the faith of Moses, and according to Talmudic doctrine had the nails on their hands and feet cut off with sharp scissors, their heads shaved, and their entire bodies washed with spring water in the same way that, according to the Law, the body and soul of a foreign woman is cleansed before she marries a Jew.

The following week Master Alodet, assistant to the Mayor of Toulouse, brought in twenty-four cartloads of Pastoureaux, whom he had seized for the massacre of 152 Jews of various ages, in Castelsarrasin and the surrounding area. By the time the carts had arrived at the castle of the Count of Narbonne, and twenty were already inside the gate, a great mob of the people of Toulouse had swarmed to the place. The Pastoureaux in the rear carts began to shout for help, claiming that they were being taken to the dungeon, although they had committed no sin but, rather, had avenged Christ's blood, which cries to the heavens for revenge. Then the mob, enraged by the injustice committed, cut the ropes the avengers were tied with, pulled them out of the carts, and shouted loudly: "Death to the Jews!" The mob poured into the Jewish quarter. I was busy reading and writing when a great number of these men burst into my chamber, armed with ignorance blunt as a whip, and hatred sharp as a knife. It wasn't my silks that brought blood to their eyes, but the books arranged on my shelves; they shoved the silks under their cloaks, but they threw the books on the floor, stamped on them, and ripped them to shreds before my eyes. Those books were bound in leather, marked with numbers, and

written by learned men; in them, had they wanted to read
them, they could have found thousands of reasons why they
should have killed me at once, and in them, had they wanted
to read them, they could also have found the balm and cure
for their hatred. I told them not to rip them apart, for many
books are not dangerous, only one is dangerous; I told them
not to tear them apart, for the reading of many books brings
wisdom, and the reading of one brings ignorance armed with
rage and hatred. But they said that everything was written in
the New Testament, that it contains all books of all times,
and therefore the rest should be burned; even if they contained something this One did not, they should be burned
all the more since they were heretical. They did not need the
advice of the learned, they said, and shouted: "Convert, or
we'll knock out of your head the wisdom from all the books
you've ever read!"

Witnessing the blind fury of this mob and seeing them
kill before my eyes the Jews who refused to be converted
(some out of faith, and others from that pride which can
sometimes be perilous), I answered that I would rather be
converted than killed, since, in spite of everything, the temporary agony of being is more valuable than the ultimate
void of nothingness. Then they seized me and pushed me
out of the house, without even allowing me to change my
house cloak for more fitting attire, and led me as I was to the
cathedral of Saint-Étienne. Two priests showed me the corpses
of Jews strewn about in front of the church; the bodies were
disfigured and the faces covered with blood. Then they
showed me a stone in front of the church, and the sight
petrified me; on the stone rested a heart, which looked like
a bloody ball. "Look," they said, "this is the heart of one
who would not be converted." A mob of people had gathered
around the heart, staring at it with astonishment and disgust.

When I closed my eyes not to see, someone hit me over the head with a rock or a whip and accelerated my decision. I said I would be converted, but I had a friend who was a priest, Brother Jean, called "the Teuton," and that I wanted him to be my godfather. I told them this, hoping that if I fell into the hands of Brother Jean, a great friend of mine, with whom I used to have long discussions on faith, perhaps he could save me from death without my having to be converted.

The two priests decided to take me out of the church and escort me to the house of Jean the Teuton because he was their superior and they feared they might do him injustice. When we came out of the church, I smelled smoke and saw flames rising over the Jewish quarter. Then they slaughtered before my eyes Asser, a twenty-year-old Jew, and said to me, "This one followed your teachings and your example." Pointing to another young man, who I later learned was from Tarascon, they said: "Your delay is killing those who believed in your teachings and followed your example." They released him, and the young man fell to the ground with his face toward me; since I had not yet uttered a word, they killed him by a deadly blow from behind. The people who were swarming in front of the church and witnessed the scene asked my escorts whether I had already converted; they said I hadn't, although, when we had started from the church, I begged them that if someone should ask, they would say that I was, but they had refused. Someone from the mob again hit me over the head with a whip, and I thought that the eyes would pop out of my head from the blow; I felt the spot, but there was no blood, only a lump, which had healed of itself, without the help of bandages, medicine, or other balms. They continued to kill Jews, and I heard their lamentations, and since the two priests told me they couldn't protect me from the fury of the mob or escort me to the house of the Confessor, because I would be killed before we reached the street, I asked them for advice. They said, "Walk the road we all walk, and we will help you." They also said, "Do not seek other paths besides the one on which everyone walks." And they also said, "Following your example, many have perished." Then I answered, "Let us return to the church."

We went back into the church, where candles were flickering and the people, their hands smeared with fresh blood, were kneeling in prayer. I asked my two keepers to wait a while longer, for I wanted to see whether my sons would come.* They waited, but when my sons didn't show up, they told me they couldn't wait any longer, and that I had to make a decision: to submit to conversion or go out to the front of the church where the undecided were still being slaughtered.

Then I told them that I would like to have the Vicar of Toulouse as my godfather, thinking of the court notary, Pierre de Savardun, one of my good friends, who could surely save me from death and conversion. I was told that the Vicar was unavailable, because that day he had brought the Pastoureaux in from Castelsarrasin, and was resting from the long journey. Some of those kneeling in the church rose up and grabbed me from all sides and pushed me toward the stone baptistry; as they forced my head under the water, I

* In connection with the above sentence, one of the modern commentators, Duvernoy, offers the following explanation: "Although the archives do not give us any information on this, we tend to interpret this statement of Baruch's not only as a delay from the painful and degrading act of conversion, but also as part of a shrewd tactic: if his sons succeeded in avoiding conversion, it was reason enough for the learned Baruch not to expose himself to their scorn; and if they were put to death, his decision would be reinforced by pain, and death would seem like redemption."

managed to utter the word "Vicar," but after that I wasn't
able to say anything; they held me under until I thought they
would drown me like a dog in the holy water of the baptistry.
Next they led me to the stone stairs and forced me to my
knees among those who were already kneeling; I don't know
how many were there or who they were, since I never looked
anyone in the face; my eyes were lowered to the stone. The
priest then performed, or so I think, all the ceremonies connected with baptism. However, before the priest began to
read the baptismal service, one of the friars bent over and
whispered into my ear that I must freely accept the ceremony
of baptism or I would be killed. So I confirmed that everything I was doing was of my free will, although I thought
otherwise. They named me Johan, or Jean; the people beside
me rose and moved away.

When all this was over, I asked the two friars to ac-
company me home, to see whether anything was left of my
possessions. They said they couldn't because they were tired
and dirty. Instead I went with them to drink wine from their
cellar in honor of my christening. I drank the wine without
saying a word; I didn't want to discuss questions of faith, although they continued to challenge me. They accompanied
me after all to my house, to see if anything was left; we found
my books mutilated and burned, my money stolen, and only
seven rolls of cloth left, some of which were pledges and
others mine, and one bedspread of Mavar silk. The friar who
now called himself my godfather put the rolls of cloth in a
sack. As we were leaving, in front of the house we ran into a
municipal official whom my recently acquired godfather
knew, and who was armed and responsible for the protection
of the Jews still alive. So my godfather told the guard: "This
one has been baptized; he is a good Christian." The guard
nodded, and I found a way to get closer to him. "Do you

want to be a good Jew?" he asked me in a whisper. I answered, "Yes." Then he said, "But do you have enough money for that?" "No," I said, "but, here, take this." I gave him the sack that contained the rolls of cloth. He handed the sack over to one of his men and said to me: "Well then, you have nothing to be afraid of, and if someone asks you, say you're a good Christian, and you'll save your head."

Some distance from my house, my godfather and I met ten municipal officials, accompanied by numerous armed guards. One of them took me aside and asked in a whisper, "Are you a Jew?" and softly, so the friar couldn't hear me, I told him that I was. This official told the friar to let me go, and handed me over to a soldier who had the rank of sergeant, ordering him to guard me as he would himself, in the name of the municipal administration and municipal authorities. The sergeant took me by the arm. When we were in the vicinity of the town hall, I told everyone who asked that I was a Jew; but when we passed through notorious narrow streets and people asked the sergeant if I wasn't perhaps a Jew who had refused baptism, he told them as I advised him: that I had been baptized and was a good Christian.

The killing and looting of the Jews lasted well into the night; the town was lit by flames, the dogs were howling on all sides. In the evening, when the streets looked deserted again, I told the sergeant that my conscience was troubling me and that I would like to go to the Vicar of Toulouse to ask him whether or not baptism accepted under the threat of death was licit. When we arrived at the Vicar's he was eating dinner, and the sergeant said in my name: "Here I've brought you a Jew who wants you personally to baptize him." The Vicar answered, "We are dining now. Sit down at the table and join us." Since I didn't want to eat, I looked around the table, and among the many guests spotted my old friend

Pierre de Savardun. I signaled to him and we stepped aside. I told him I didn't intend to undergo baptism, and asked him to tell the Vicar not to force me, since such a baptism would not be licit. He did this for me, and whispered my words into the Vicar's ear. Then he told the sergeant to go, for now he himself would guard me. He handed me over to another sergeant, one of his trusted men, with whom I was to go to the castle of Narbonne, to see if any of my sons were among the slaughtered Jews whose bodies were kept in the castle's yard. When we came back to the table, the Vicar asked me: "Do you want to be baptized now or would you rather wait until tomorrow?" Then Pierre de Savardun took him aside and discussed something with him in a confidential tone. I don't know exactly what he told him, but the Vicar replied: "Naturally I don't wish to baptize anyone by force, whether he be a Jew or anyone else." From that I concluded that the baptism to which I had been subjected by force could be considered invalid.

When this was resolved, I asked Pierre de Savardun for advice: should I stay on in the castle of Narbonne or leave? Since Pierre told me that all Jews who took shelter in the castle would be either baptized or killed, we decided that I should leave for Toulouse. Pierre gave me three shillings and accompanied me to the crossroads, from where the main road leads to Montgiscard. He told me to walk as fast as possible, and to speak only German if I met anyone.

So I hurried to reach Montgiscard as soon as possible. When I finally arrived and was crossing the town square, suddenly a mob of people armed with whips and knives poured out of nowhere, seized me, and asked me whether I was a Jew or a Christian. I asked them to tell me who they were themselves, and they said, "We are the devout Pastoureaux, in the service of Christ's Faith." They also said to me, "In the name of the paradise of both heaven and earth, we shall exterminate all those who do not follow His road, both Jews and non-Jews." I told them that I was not a Jew and said to them: "Can the paradise of heaven and earth be reached by blood and flames?" And they replied: "Even a single unbelieving soul is enough to deprive us all of hope and paradise, as one mangy sheep is enough to infect the entire flock." They also said, "Isn't it better to slaughter one mangy sheep than to allow the whole flock to become tainted?" And they shouted, "Arrest him! His words reek of doubt and disbelief!" So they bound my wrists and took me away. I also asked them, "Is your power over people such that you can dispose of their freedom?" And they said, "We are Christ's soldiers, and have final authority to separate the diseased from the healthy, the infidel from the faithful."

Then I told them that faith was born of doubt and I told them that doubt was my faith, and that I was a Jew, because I hoped they wouldn't kill me with my hands bound. The mob now dispersed, not caring for learned discussion and dialectic, and instead went toward a certain dark street where they had caught another victim. They took me to a large house and lowered me into the cavernous cellars, where there were some ten Jews, including the learned Bernardo Lupo and his daughter, called "La Bonne" because of her goodness. We spent the night and the next day in prayer, and decided that we wouldn't let them baptize us, but would persist in our own faith. Our prayer was interrupted only by rats, which, heavy and well fed, were squeaking in the corners and running around the cellar all night long. The next day they brought us out and sent us under guard to Mazères and from there to Pamiers.*

* By the decree of Arnaud Dejean, the Inquisitor of Pamiers, in the diocese of Pamiers, the Jews had the right to live in freedom. This decree, of March 2,

"Did you revert to the Jewish faith in Pamiers or anywhere else, and according to the Law of Moses?"

"No. Under Talmudic doctrine, only when someone is converted willingly and by Christian rules, and then wants to revert to his old faith again, must he submit to the procedure I have already described—the cutting of nails and hair, and washing of the entire body—since he is considered unclean. But when he is not converted willingly and according to all the Christian rules, but by force, then this procedure doesn't apply, and such a conversion is considered invalid."

"Did you tell one or more persons who were baptized under the threat of death that their conversion was invalid, so that they could, unpunished and in peace, revert to Judaism?"

"No. Except for what I said a while ago about Solomon and Eleazar."

"Did you tell one or more Jews to accept baptism only to avoid death and afterward to revert to Judaism?"

"No."

"Were you ever present at the ceremony of the return of a converted Jew to Moses' faith?"

"No."

"Do you consider your own conversion invalid?"

"Yes."

"Why do you willingly expose yourself to the danger of heresy?"

"Because I wish to live in peace with myself and not with the world."

"Explain."

1298, which forbade the inhabitants and the civil authority to treat the Jews "too sternly and cruelly," shows the degree to which the personal attitude and courage of the inhabitants could in hard times change that fate which cowards believe to be inevitable and pronounce to be fate and historical necessity.

"Since I don't know what Christians believe and why, since on the other hand I do know what Jews believe and why, and since I consider their faith to be proven by the Law and the Prophetic Books, which I have studied as a doctor for some twenty years, I say that, until it is proven to me by my Law and my Prophets that the Christian faith conforms to them, I will not believe in Christianity, despite the security offered me in the fold of that faith. I would rather die than abandon my faith."

This was the beginning of the debate over Christian faith with Baruch David Neumann, who continued to resist with the strength of his arguments, while the Most Venerable Father in Christ, Monsignor Jacques, by the grace of God Bishop of Pamiers, showed boundless patience in bringing the said Baruch to the Truth, sparing neither time nor effort. The Jew, however, obstinately clung to his belief, relying on the Old Testament and rejecting the light of Christian faith which Monsignor Jacques was so mercifully bestowing on him.

On August 16, 1330, Baruch finally wavered, confessed, and affirmed that he had renounced the Jewish faith. Since they had read to him the record of the hearing, the said Neumann, when asked whether he had made his confession under torture or immediately thereafter, answered that he had made his confession immediately thereafter, about three o'clock in the morning, and on that same day in the evening hours he made the same confession without having been first brought into the torture chamber.

This hearing took place in the presence of Monsignor Jacques, by the grace of God Bishop of Pamiers, Friar Gaillard de Pamiers, the Magistrate Bernard Faissasier, the Magistrate David de Troyes, a Jew, and us, Guillaume-Pierre

Barthes and Robert de Robecourt, notaries of the Inquisitor of Carcassonne.

It is known that Baruch David Neumann appeared before the same tribunal on two more occasions: the first, in the middle of May of the following year, when he declared that after a rereading of the Law and the Prophets he had again swayed in his faith. There followed a long debate over the Hebrew sources; the patient and prolonged arguments of Monsignor Jacques led Baruch again to renounce Judaism. The final sentence carries the date of November 20, 1337. The record of the hearing, however, has not been preserved, and Duvernoy offers the logical hypothesis that the unfortunate Baruch had most likely died under torture. Another source tells of a certain Baruch who was sentenced for the same offense of thinking and burned at the stake some twenty years later. It is difficult to imagine that this reference is to the same person.

A NOTE

The story of Baruch David Neumann is actually a translation of the third chapter of the *Registers of the Inquisition* (*Confessio Baruc olim iudei modo baptizati et post modum reversi ad iudaismum*), in which Jacques Fournier, the future Pope Benedict XII, entered scrupulously and in detail the confessions and testimony given before his tribunal. The manuscript is preserved in the Fondi Latini of the Vatican Library, number 4030. I have made only certain minor omissions in the text, where there is a discussion of the Holy Trinity, Christ as the Messiah, the Fulfillment of the Word of the Law, and the denial of certain assertions of the Old Testament. The translation is based on the French version by Monsignor Jean-Marie Vidal, former vicar of the church of Saint Louis in Rome, as well as on the version of the Catholic exegete, the Honorable Ignacio von Döllinger, published in Munich in 1890. These texts, with their useful and learned commentaries, have been reprinted many times—most recently, as far as I know, in 1965. The original manuscript ("a beautiful parchment scroll with a scribal hand in two columns") reaches the reader as a triple echo of a distant voice—Baruch's, if we include his voice in the translation, like a reverberation of Yahweh's thought.

The sudden accidental discovery of this text, the discovery that coincided with the happy completion of the story entitled "A Tomb for Boris Davidovich," left me with a feeling of miraculous illumination: the analogy with the story already told is obvious to such a degree that I see the identical motives, dates, and names as God's part in creation, *la part de Dieu,* or the devil's, *la part du diable.*

The consistency of moral beliefs; the spilling of the sacrificial blood; the similarity in names (Boris Davidovich Novsky; Baruch David Neumann); the coincidence in dates of the arrests of Novsky and Neumann (on the same day of the fatal month of December, but with a span of six centuries: 1330–1930)—all this suddenly appeared in my consciousness as an enlarged metaphor of the classical doctrine of the cyclic movement of time: "He who has seen the present has seen everything, that which happened in the most distant past and that which will happen in the future" (Marcus Aurelius, *Meditations,* Book VI, 37). Polemicizing with the Stoics (and even more so with Nietzsche), J. L. Borges formulates their teachings as follows: "From time to time the world is destroyed by the flame that created it, and then is born again to experience the same history. Again the same molecular particles fuse, again they give form to stones, trees, people—even to virtues and days, because for the Greeks there is no noun without substance. Again each sword and each hero, again each trivial sleepless night."

In this context the sequence of *variability* is without great significance. Nevertheless, I chose the sequence of spiritual rather than historical dates: as I have said, I discovered the history of David Neumann after writing the story of Boris Davidovich.

THE SHORT BIOGRAPHY OF A. A. DARMOLATOV

1892–1968

In our time when many poets' destinies are shaped according to the monstrous standard model of epoch, class, and environment, and when the fatal facts of life—the unique magic of the first poem, the journey to exotic Tiflis for the jubilee of Rustaveli, or the meeting with the one-armed poet Narbut—are reduced to a chronological sequence without the flavor of adventure and blood, the biography of A. A. Darmolatov, though somewhat sketchy, is not without a lyrical core. Out of the confused mass of facts, there emerges a naked human life.

Under the influence of his father, a village teacher who was an amateur biologist and chronic alcoholic, Darmolatov was fascinated by the secrets of nature from an early age. On their landed estate (his mother's dowry) in the small town of Nikolaevski, the dogs, birds, and cats lived in relative freedom. In his sixth year, in nearby Saratov they bought him Devrienne's *Atlas of the Butterflies of Europe and Central Asia,* one of the last valuable works of engraving of the

nineteenth century. At seven, he assisted his father in dissect-
ing rodents and performing experiments on frogs. At ten,
reading novels of the Spanish-American War, he became a
passionate defender of the Spaniards, and at twelve he hid a
wafer under his tongue, brought it out of the church, and put
it down on the bench before his dumbfounded friends. Reading the texts of Korch, he dreamed of ancient times, despising
the present. There could be nothing, therefore, more typical
than this provincial environment and this positivistically edu-
cated middle class; nothing more banal than this heredity,
combining alcoholism and tuberculosis on the father's side
with the melancholic depression of the mother, a reader of
French novels. Also on the mother's side was an aunt, Yad-
viga Yarmolaevna, who was living with them and slowly
drifting into dementia—the only respectable fact in the poet's
early biography.

On the eve of the First Revolution his mother suddenly
died; she fell asleep over Maeterlinck's *The Life of the Bee,*
which stayed open in her lap, like a dead bird. The same year,
fertilized by the semen of death, Darmolatov's first verses
appeared in the publication *Life and School,* which was put
out by Saratov's circle of young revolutionaries. In 1912, he
enrolled in St. Petersburg's university, where, following his
father's wish, he studied medicine. Already, between 1912
and 1915, he was being published in the capital's reviews:
Education, The Contemporary World, and the glorious
Apollo. At about this time we have to place his acquaintance
with Gorodetsky, and with the poet-suicide Victor Hoffman,
who, as Makovsky said, had lived as a man and died as a poet,
shooting himself with a tiny ladies' Browning through the
eye, like some lyrical Cyclops. Darmolatov's first and undoubtedly best collection, *Ores and Crystals,* appeared in
1915, in the old orthography and with the face of Atalanta

on its cover. "In this not very extensive collection," wrote an anonymous reviewer in *The Word,* "there is something of the mastery of an Innokenty Annensky, a youthful sincerity of feeling in the spirit of Baratynski, a certain radiance as in young Bunin. But there is no true fervor in it, no true mastery, no sincere feeling, though no particular weak spots either."

It is not my intention here to concern myself closely with the poetic qualities of Darmolatov, or to enter into the complex mechanism of literary fame. Nor are the poet's war adventures of any importance to this story, though I confess that certain vivid pictures from Galicia and Bukovina during Brusilov's offensive—when the cadet Darmolatov, an assistant medical officer, discovered the butchered body of his brother—are not without attraction. Nor is his Berlin excursion without charm, or his sentimental adventure, which, against the background of the starved and tragic Russia of the civil war, ended with a honeymoon in the hell of Kislovodsk. His poetry, regardless of what the critics say, offers a plenitude of empirical (poetic) facts, which, like old post cards or photographs in a shabby album, testify as much to his travels, ecstasies, and passions as to literary fashion: the beneficent influence of the wind on the marble clusters of caryatids; the Tiergarten lined with flowering linden trees; the lanterns of the Brandenburg Gate; the monstrous apparitions of the black swans; the rosy reflection of the sun on the murky waters of the Dnieper; the spell of white nights; the magical eyes of Circassian women; a knife plunged to the hilt into the ribs of a wolf of the steppes; the spin of an airplane propeller; the caw of the crow in the early dusk; a snapshot (from a bird's-eye view) of the terrible panorama of ravaged Povolozh; the creeping of tractors and threshers through the golden wheat of the prairies; the black shafts of Kursk coal

mines; the towers of the Crimea in the ocean of air; the purple velvet of theater boxes; the ghostly figures of bronze
statues flashing amid fireworks; the sweep of ballerinas spun
of foam; the splendor of the petroleum flame from the tanker
in the harbor; the horrible narcosis of rhymes; the still life of
a cup of tea, a silver spoon, and a drowned wasp; the violet
eyes of the harnessed horse; the optimistic grinding of turbine
engines; the head of the commander Frunze on an operating
table amid the intoxicating smell of chloroform; the bare
trees in Lubyanka's yard; the hoarse howling of village dogs;
the wondrous balance of cement piles; the stalking of a cat
following the trail of a winter bird in the snow; grainfields
under a barrage of artillery fire; the lovers' parting in the
valley of the Kama; the military cemetery near Sevastopol ...

The poems dated 1918 and 1919 offer no hint of their
place of origin: in them everything still occurs in the cosmopolitan region of the soul, which has no precise map. In 1921
we find him in St. Petersburg, in the somber opulence of the
former palace of the Yeliseyevs, in that Ship of Fools, as
Olga Forsh says, to which the starving brotherhood of poets
without any income or clear orientation had flocked. According to Makovsky, in those birds of God only their lunatic
eyes, with a frenzied gleam, were alive. They earnestly tried
to look alive, he says, although you couldn't shake the feeling,
despite the glaring lipstick of the women, that you were moving among phantoms. Outside, the furious storm was raging,
driven by the magnetic poles of revolution-counterrevolution:
at the cost of insane daring, Bukhara again fell into the hands
of the Bolsheviks; the mutiny of Kronstadt's sailors was
crushed in a sea of blood; around the ravaged settlements
human shells were dragging themselves—helpless women
with gangrenous legs, and children with swollen bellies;
when the nags, dogs, cats, and rats had been exterminated,

barbaric cannibalism became the unwritten law. "Who are we with, we Serapion Brothers?" shouted Leo Lunz. "We are with the hermit Serapion!" As far as he was concerned, Kruchenykh was for mindlessness: "Mindlessness awakens one and gives free rein to the creative imagination, without having to contend with anything concrete." "We are making it possible for our fellow poets to have total freedom in their choice of creative methods, providing..." the smithy group added. (Accepted unanimously, with one abstention.)

In a photograph from that period, Darmolatov still has the appearance of a St. Petersburg dandy, with dickey and bow tie. Gaunt, "with eyes staring at the ruins of Rome," with a chin slashed by a dimple that looks like a scar, with lips tightly pressed, his face reveals nothing, resembles a stony mask. Reliable documents indicate that at that time the young Darmolatov had already accepted the cosmopolitan program of the Acmeists. This "longing for European culture" was primarily inspired in him by another poet, Mandelstam: both equally respected Rome, Annensky, and Gumilev and devoured them, like sweets, with hysterical greed.

One hot August evening in that same year of 1921, an orgy was in progress at the Yeliseyev palace, which Olga Forsh, with typical feminine exaggeration, called "a feast amid the plague." Their standard fare in those years was salted fish with draughts of horrible *samogon*, prepared according to alchemical recipes combining methyl alcohol, birch bark, and pepper. That evening "Cassandra" (Anna Andreyevna Akhmatova) was under the spell of one of her prophetic intuitions; from the peak of ecstasy she suddenly fell into a sick depression bordering on hallucination. It isn't known who brought the news of the execution of the "master," Gumilev, but it is certain that this news passed like a small, isolated magnetic storm through all these antagonistic groups separated by distinct ideological and aesthetic programs. A glass in hand and stumbling drunkenly, Darmolatov left Cassandra's table and threw himself in the gaping shabby armchair of the deceased Yeliseyev, next to the proletarian writer Dorogoychenko.

In July 1930, he was staying at the Suhumsky Rest Home, working on translations commissioned by the journal *Red News* at the suggestion of Boris Davidovich Novsky. At the beginning of his acquaintance with Novsky, there was a distant Berlin encounter in a café near the Tiergarten, when the young Darmolatov listened with awe, admiration, and fear to the bold prophesies of Tverdohlebov—in other words, B. D. Novsky, the future commissar of the Revolutionary Naval Committee, diplomat, representative of the People's Commissariat for Communications and Liaisons. They say that in relatively lean times Novsky was his "connection"—a word indicating the complex bond between poets and the government whereby, on the basis of personal sympathies and sentimental debts of youth, the rigidity of the revolutionary line was softened. (Such a bond was greatly entangled and full of danger: if the powerful protector fell into disfavor, all the protégés rolled down the steep hill after him, as if carried by lava set in motion by the scream of the unlucky one.)

In late December, two days after Novsky's arrest, the telephone rang in Darmolatov's house. It was exactly 3:00 A.M. The receiver was picked up by Darmolatov's groggy wife, a pregnant Tartar, with a high, bulging belly. At the other end there was only a terrifying silence that makes one's blood freeze. The woman replaced the receiver and burst into tears. From then on, the telephone in his apartment was muffled by multicolored feather pillows covered with flashy decorative motifs full of the flamboyant noise of Tartar fairs, while beside the desk, burdened with manuscripts, dictionaries, and books that he was translating "for his nerves," stood a cardboard suitcase, packed and ready for sudden departure. Once, emboldened by vodka, he had even shown this suitcase to a poet-informer: on top of the warm knitted sweater and flannel underwear lay a leather-bound copy of Ovid's elegies in Latin. In those days, the verses of that famous exile must have sounded to him like Pushkin's motto about his own poetic destiny.

At the beginning of the next year, he traveled to Georgia; in May, he published a cycle of poems entitled *Tiflis in One's Hands;* in September, he was placed on the Writers' Request List and received, through an order signed by Gorky, a pair of trousers, a lined coat, and a beaver hat. (It seems that Darmolatov refused this fur hat because of its "hetman appearance." Aleksei Maksimovich had insisted he shouldn't be so choosy! In light of all the versions in circulation about this event, it is difficult to know what Gorky really said, but it seems that he made some allusion to Darmolatov's hot head, and the latter "almost died like one of Chekov's clerks.")

On August 17, 1933, a photograph shows him on the ship *J. V. Stalin,* among some hundred and twenty writers who had just visited the recently completed White Sea–Baltic canal. Darmolatov has turned old overnight, and wears sideburns à la Pushkin. In a white suit and an unbuttoned shirt, he leans on the deck railing, staring into space. The wind blows through Vera Inber's hair. Bruno Yasensky (the second from the left) raises his hand toward the invisible foggy shore. With his hand cupped to his ear, Zoshchenko tries to make out the melody played by the band. The sounds are scattered by the wind and the noise of the water spilling over the floodgate.

His appearance notwithstanding, there are irrefutable proofs that Darmolatov was at this time in the grip of a psychological malady: he washed his hands in methyl alcohol and saw an informer in everyone. They persistently visited him, unannounced and without knocking, wearing colorful cravats, like lovers of poetry, or like translators, bringing miniature Eiffel Towers made of gold tin, or like plumbers, with enormous guns in their back pockets instead of plungers.

In November, he arrived at the hospital, where they treated him with sleep cures: he slept through five full weeks in the sterile landscape of hospital rooms, and from that time on it was as if worldly clamor could never reach him again. Even the terrible ukulele of the poet Kirsanov, on the other side of the partition, was muffled by cotton covered with a thin layer of ear ointment. At the intervention of the Writers Union, he was given permission to visit the town's stables twice a week; they would see him, awkward and heavy, with the first signs of elephantiasis, riding a tame horse from the stables at a trot. Before Mandelstam's departure for Samatiha (where prison and destruction awaited him), he and his wife dropped in to say good-bye to Darmolatov. They found him in front of the elevator in a funny riding habit with a child's tiny whip in his hand. A taxi had just arrived and he hurried away to the stables, without saying good-bye to his childhood friend.

In the summer of 1947, he arrived at Cetinje, in Montenegro, for the jubilee of *The Mountain Wreath*, fragments of which, it seems, he was translating. Although well on in years, ungainly and clumsy, he stepped lightly over the red silk ribbon separating Njegoš's gigantic chair, which looked like the throne of a god, from the poets and mortals. I who am telling this story stood to one side and watched the uninvited poet squirming in Njegoš's high austere chair; taking advantage of the applause, I slipped out of the portrait gallery in order not to witness the scandal that the intervention of my uncle, the museum curator, would cause. But I distinctly remember that between the poet's spread legs, under his threadbare pants, the horrible swelling was already visible.

Before the terrible disease tied him to his bed, he spent the last year of his life quietly, chewing the sweet cud of his youth. He used to visit Anna Andreyevna, and once, they say, he brought her a flower.

POSTSCRIPT

He remains a medical phenomenon in Russian literature: Darmolatov's case was entered in all the latest pathology textbooks. A photograph of his scrotum, the size of the biggest collective farm pumpkin, is also reprinted in foreign medical books, wherever elephantiasis (elephantiasis nostras) *is mentioned, and as a moral for writers that to write one must have more than big balls.*